LORDS
OF
ATLANTIS

LORDS OF ATLANTIS

WALLACE WEST

AIRMONT PUBLISHING COMPANY, INC.
22 EAST 60TH STREET • NEW YORK 22

LORDS OF ATLANTIS

An AIRMONT BOOK published by arrangement with Thomas Bouregy and Company, Inc.

PRINTING HISTORY

Bouregy edition published June, 1960
Airmont edition published October, 1963

PUBLISHED SIMULTANEOUSLY IN THE DOMINION OF CANADA
BY THE RYERSON PRESS, TORONTO

PRINTED IN THE UNITED STATES OF AMERICA
BY THE COLONIAL PRESS INC., CLINTON, MASSACHUSETTS

LORDS
OF
ATLANTIS

Chapter 1

There were giants in the earth in those days and also after that, when the sons of God came in unto the daughters of men and they bare children unto them, the same became mighty men which were of old, men of renown . . . *Genesis,* 6-4.

Teraf, Prince of Hellas, pressed his straight nose against a promenade deck porthole of the *Poseidon* as the liner drifted earthward at the end of her record-breaking run from Mars. Within half an hour the *Poseidon* would be docked at Atlan, but she was still so high that the capital of colonial Atlantis looked like a white button on the green silk of the Mediterranean valley.

Far to the east, Teraf could just make out the brown deserts of Arabia. Northward were the mountains of his own Hellas and he thought he glimpsed the marble porticoes of Athens gleaming in the sunlight.

To the westward, on the very edge of the horizon, lay a faint blue line which must be the Atlantic coast. The prince strained his eyes in an effort to catch sight of the mammoth dam between the Pillars of Heracles, but the distance was too great. Over all that expanse, masses of thunderheads were drifting, for it was the season of summer showers.

"Probably get a wetting when we land," Teraf commented idly to a passenger who had preempted a nearby porthole.

"Think of it," chirped the other, who looked like a college professor back from vacation. "And we had to beg for bath water on Mars. Ah, if only they had some of this precipitation there!" The little fellow moved to a better vantage point and Teraf was left to his own reflections.

"Same old town," he mused, staring down at the marble towers, fairy gardens and circular canals which were now hidden, now revealed by the hurrying clouds. "Same old people, too, I'll bet. Zeus Pitar's gout will be a little worse than when I left. Hera will be a little fatter but still fussing with her court receptions. Aphrodite? Well . . ." He gasped and grabbed for a stanchion as the *Poseidon's* pilot, deciding to risk the storm, cut out most of the gravity screens and allowed the ship to drop like a rock into the fleecy darkness of the clouds.

In a moment they were through. Now Atlan lay close beneath them, wet and shining, like a newly-cleansed jewel. Then the thousand-foot-long ship bumped gently on its runway and came to rest with a groan like that of a tired living thing.

The doors of the promenade deck unscrewed with a sigh of compressed air and Earth-hungry passengers began streaming out on the dock, followed by puffing stewards bearing their baggage. That, of course, was the moment when the clouds opened and sent sheets of rain sweeping across the unprotected drome.

Pulling his helmet down over his red hair, and swinging his elbows ruthlessly, Teraf tried to dodge through the crowd and escape the committee which, he was sure, Hera had sent to welcome him. But it was no use; an officer whom he had failed to bribe pointed him out and a group of officials in bedraggled scarlet cloaks drew themselves up before him. "Welcome, Prince Teraf of Hellas!" proclaimed the spokesman, a dried-up wisp of humanity whom the new arrival remembered vaguely as Doctor Vanya, physician, high priest and official greeter of the Atlantean court. Zeus Pitar sends his regrets that ill-health prevented his being here in person to welcome you and bids you wait upon him in the royal suite of the royal . . ."

"Hey, Prince! Prince!" someone was bawling above the roaring rain and the screams of the scurrying crowd. Then the owner of the voice, a lean and lanky youngster in civilian harness, thrust his dripping bronze figure through the mob and grabbed Teraf by the arm.

"Sorry, Prince," he apologized as Vanya and the other committeemen drew themselves up in soggy hauteur. "Hate to bother you, but I'm Hermes of the *Evening Planet*. The boys want a photograph and I want an interview. If you'll just step this way . . ."

Teraf somehow found himself facing a battery of lenses while the usual banter common to newspapermen the universe over, was tossed back and forth.

"Have a rough crossing?" demanded one. "How's it feel to brush a comet's tail?"

"It never touched us." The prince laughed that one off.

"Do you think the comet will hit Earth?" chirped another reporter. "We understand . . ."

"You'll have to ask the captain that one," parried Teraf.

"Do you think Terran girls are prettier than . . ."

Hermes finally rescued the perspiring prince and returned him to the fidgeting reception committee, after exacting a promise for an exclusive interview later.

Under the wing of the fussy little doctor, the new arrival was hustled down a landing dock elevator and into the official car.

Between polite comments to members of his escort, as the car glided along its repulsion rails into the heart of the city, Teraf had time to survey the town. The ten years of his sojourn on Mars had made little appreciable change. Atlan still looked like the prosperous colonial capital it was, but the buildings of white marble looked smaller and the streets narrower than he remembered them.

Also, the sprinkling of red-haired, tall and deep-chested Martians seemed almost lost in the press of blond Hellenes, dark-skinned Arabs and bearded Northmen which filled the sidewalks.

Teraf was especially struck by the appearance of the transplanted Martians and compared them unfavorably with the pale, graceful citizens back "home," as the red planet was always referred to. The rays of the Earthly sun had burned their sensitive skins almost as black as those of the Nubians who occasionally wended their way through the crowds. And to meet the stress of Terran gravitation they had developed enormous muscles, which sat poorly on their slender frames and gave them the deceitful appearance of strong men in a circus. In other words, they didn't quite fit.

The Alfhas—those of mixed Martian and Earthly parentage—apparently had absorbed the best traits of both races, he observed, tingling with pride because he was one of the latter. These Alfhas, of whom there were a great number on the streets, had the blazing hair and slim grace of their Martian forebears, plus a better adaptation to Earthly conditions, inherited from their Terran blood.

The Crooked Mountain, on which the Pitar's palace was located now loomed squat and ugly before them like a nightcap dropped on the plain. The silver tracery of the Bab El radio tower graced its summit like a spider's web while the creamy structures in which beat the official heart of Atlantis peeped from amidst the green of its olive groves.

As the car skimmed a bridge which spanned the second of the city's five circular canals, the prince caught sight of the racecourse which was the pride of Atlan. The results of races there were even flashed to Mars. He had bet on them many a time.

Crossing another bridge they swept into the business section with its colorful shops, block-square combines and squat, windowless warehouses. In the latter, he knew, were stored the priceless cargoes of merchandise which dropped upon Atlan from all corners of Earth.

The fourth circle, which housed the barracks and parade

grounds of the army, was not in that state of busting activity which characterized the rest of the city. The frowning marble fortresses, armed with their squat infra-heat guns, seemed almost deserted. Only a few guards loitered about the approaches to the last bridge.

A three-minute glide through carefully tended parkland brought them at last to the Inner Island and to the pillared façade of the Pitarichal palace from which Zeus ruled the world and conversed with the stars. Here there were soldiers in plenty, standing stiffly at attention in two long lines at either side of the entrance. Through this lane of honor, Vanya and his fellows proudly escorted the prince into the reception hall.

Teraf's nose wrinkled a little at this ostentation. *That's what comes of having an ambitious, stupid wife,* he reflected, comparing the almost barbaric splendor of the chamber with the simple dignity of similar rooms at Minos, capital of the Martian Anarchiate. Zeus must be coming more and more under Hera's influence, he concluded. Time for a young man to take over the Pitarship if he, Teraf, knew anything about it.

But the prince's attitude changed somewhat when he saw that, except for a few officials who were passing busily back and forth, the reception room was empty. He was to be let off without a formal welcome then? He wondered.

With a flourish, Dr. Vanya ushered him into the Pitar's private chamber and withdrew wistfully, leaving Teraf alone with the mighty Zeus himself. The Pitar was swathed in a toga of sky blue silk and had his bad foot propped upon a padded stool. His secretary, a strikingly handsome youth, assisted him to arise when the visitor was announced.

"Welcome home, Teraf," the governor of Atlantis smiled through his bushy red beard as he limped forward with outstretched hands. "Remembering how you used to hate court occasions, I begged off this morning on account of my foot."

"Your gout is worse then?" asked the prince to make conversation.

"It's damned painful. Wish I could get a leave of absence and go home for a while. This damp climate is killing me . . . Apollo, get us a flagon of nectar, like a good boy."

As the secretary withdrew, Zeus slipped his arm around his visitor's shoulders and led him to a windowseat which overlooked the capital and the distance-misted mountains of Crete. The Pitar sank into the cushions with a grunt of relief and, picking up the jagged scepter which was the symbol of his power, began tracing complicated patterns with it on the rug.

"You'll stay in your old room at the palace, of course," he said at last. "Glad you arrived in time to attend the reception and conclave of the ten governors of Atlantis tonight. The old summer solstice rigmarole, you know, but I've still got to give the barbarians pomp and circumstance, auguries and tokens, ambrosia and horseraces or they become grumpy.

"That's really why I humor Hera when she wants to give a reception, you know. She thinks such things are necessary and she should know. At heart she's a barb—" He stopped himself with a slight cough. "You'll not have to sit beside the altar tonight unless that brother of yours fails to show up, so you can get away early.

"How are things back home?" he changed the subject after a pause. There was wistfulness in his mellow bass voice.

"Just about the same," replied the prince, who was regaining that sense of ease with which, in his youth, he had conversed with his strange paradox of a Pitar, whose cleancut mouth was always ready to smile at a friend and whose bright little eyes could sparkle equally at a jest or the sight of a pretty woman.

"They're running a new canal from the South Pole to the Equator," Teraf continued. "I suppose you've read of it in the dispatches. Half a mile wide. It will use every drop of water from the ice cap. I worked on it all this year getting my engineering degree."

Zeus nodded, though his eyes were fastened anxiously on the window and the slowly clearing skies.

"It's a continual fight all the time. Everybody's on food and water rations now. Chemical food, mostly. Brrr! And Earth may be damp but you should be glad you're down here where one doesn't have to send in a requisition in order to take a bath."

"Yes, life up there is a struggle," the Pitar admitted, "but it's no picnic down here either just now. We could use twice as many immigrants if they could be spared from canal building. We're terribly short of soldiers, too—just when the natives are all worked up about this comet business. They think it's a portent. Someone—I don't know who—yet," his jaw tightened and he gave the rug a vicious jab, "is trying to use their fear to break down confidence in the government. There's even talk of a revolution . . ."

"Nonsense," laughed Teraf, wondering suddenly if the old man was entering his dotage. "I'm sure . . ."

"I suppose," interrupted the Pitar, "that observers on the *Poseidon* were watching the comet. What did they make of it?"

"Had them worried for a while." Teraf took one of the glasses of nectar which Apollo returned to proffer at that moment. "If we had been delayed we might have been hit, you know, since the comet is cutting right between the orbits of Mars and Earth. The ship set a new speed record on account of it. Three weeks and two days. Not bad for 90,000,000 miles."

"Did the observers think there was any danger either to Earth or Mars?" Zeus neglected his own drink to peer out through the window from which the new celestial body could now be seen rising over the horizon. Its ruddy light was clearly visible, despite the fact that the sun was almost at the zenith.

"They didn't think so. The comet has a considerable body of solid material in the head. In fact, it's about the size and density of Earth. But it should miss us by some 17,000,000 miles. At that distance it can only disturb the tides and perhaps alter our orbit a very little."

"Well, if that's all," sighed the Pitar, "maybe there'll be no trouble." He gulped his drink and held out his glass for another. "Perhaps I shouldn't tell you this," he continued after waving his secretary away, "but as next in line for the throne of Hellas, I think you ought to know." His widely-spaced gray eyes looked into Teraf's blue ones for a long moment.

"We're sitting on top of a volcano, my boy," he said at last. "I have made the mistake of thinking that Earthlings would appreciate the benefits they receive from our rule—better living conditions, education, longer life, no wars.

"Instead, they are a bunch of ungrateful brutes." His voice was bitter. "Excuse me, I know you're half Earthling, but I believe you can be trusted. As for your brother Refo—I don't know. I don't know." The Pitar brought himself up with a start.

"Enough of this," he grumbled, starting to rise and then subsiding with a groan as his gouty foot protested. "You must want a bath in some of that water you feel so strongly toward. Just be sure you're on hand for the conclave, and keep your eyes and ears open. The ten governors should all be there. Your brother is flying in from Athens . . . why he couldn't have been here to greet you I don't know."

He touched a bell. Apollo returned and helped his master

to arise. Zeus then escorted his guest to the door and turned him over to Vanya, who still hovered outside.

Deep in thought over what he had just heard, Teraf trudged slowly through the gracious, softly illuminated halls. Things were not the same as when he had left Atlantis. He sighed and became conscious of Earth's gravitational pull.

It was the old story, he reflected. The same thing that had got Martians in trouble so many times before—assuming that half-savages were moved by the same high principles as themselves. He had read in the history books of the first tragic attempt to colonize Earth thousands of years before. And then there was the fiasco on Venus. Were the Martians too soft? Too generous? Would they be left to smother gallantly on their little planet in the end? He thrust out his firm chin and startled Dr. Vanya by swearing that it would not be so this time if he could help it.

When they reached the well-remembered high carved door in the east wing, Vanya was all for coming in and making his prince comfortable with his own hands. Teraf succeeded in shooing him away and entered his room alone.

The apartment was vast, yet simple and to his taste. He had often stayed there when, with his tall, silent father, he had paid his first visits to the capital. Teraf was startled out of his reverie by a voice issuing from a chair which had been drawn up before one of the windows.

"Come in, prince," it said, "and make yourself at home, same as I have."

Reclining on the small of his back, with his feet on the windowsill, a glass of nectar in one hand and a slice of ambrosia in the other was Hermes, he of the *Evening Planet.* His smile was so infectious that Teraf found his somber humor lightening. It was impossible to be annoyed with his grinning, freckled intruder.

"I'd get up and tap my eyebrows if I were a gentleman," grumbled the reporter as he squinted up at the prince, judging and weighing him through his mockery. "However, there are too many gentlemen in this dump as it is. Wipe the grime of space travel off your face and then pull up a chair. I want to talk."

A valet who had been lurking in the background now led the way to the bedroom where clean harness had been laid out and a bath drawn.

Returning half an hour later, Teraf found his guest apparently in deep slumber with the empty goblet dangling from his long fingers. But it was not so.

"You are now a credit to Atlan," Hermes declared, surveying through one half-closed eye the trim figure in linen trunks, loose shirt and sandals which confronted him. "Pardon my rudeness again. I've been working day and night on this comet story until I'm asleep on my feet. Besides, I'm half-shot on your nectar." He pulled himself three vertebrae higher in the chair.

Teraf ordered more wine while, with the ease of a star newsman, Hermes led the conversation into devious channels. What were the prince's impressions of Mars after ten years there? Was he returning to Hellas at once? What did he hope to accomplish in that godforsaken place with his civil engineering? What did he think of the comet? Was he planning to marry? And finally, what were his impressions of Earth after such a long absence?

To the latter question, Teraf replied that he could make no answer other than to comment upon the increased number of barbarians on the streets of Atlan.

"That's just the point," exclaimed Hermes, suddenly vibrating with excitement. "That's my lead. That's just what I wanted you to say. Look! Atlan used to be a Martian city. Old Poseidon laid it out after he conquered Atlantis, in a manner which made it impregnable. Five moats encircling the town . . . fortresses . . . all that. He knew a thing or two about colonization, that boy. Then he had to go and get himself killed when a mere infant—125 years old, wasn't he? And they went and picked Zeus to succeed him.

"Now Zeus is all right," the chronicler hastened to add, "but he trusts everybody. He has turned the army into an engineering corps, planted colonies all over the map and let the barbarians pour in here from every direction. We Martians are becoming as scarce as sabertooth tigers.

"Great Land of Nod!" Hermes was sitting bold upright now. "I've been traveling around this town getting the reaction on the comet. The place is a regular hotbed of rebellion. The Gauls and Britons, who were brought here to work in the factories, are aching for loot. You should see their hungry eyes when they pass a shop . . . or a pretty girl."

Hermes poured himself another glass of nectar and continued his monologue in a slightly thickening voice.

"You can't transform a savage into a civilized human being in a century, Prinsh." He wagged his burnished head gravely. "You've got to hammer the tar out of him until he becomes afraid to turn pirate every time your back is turned. The Pitar is too easy. He thinks too much of the Martian's burden, and not enough of the Martian's scalp."

"Wait a minute," Teraf broke in, "are you arguing that we enslave these people?"

"Don't hand me that stuff. Every colonial people is enslaved. What do you think we've got colonies on Earth for? They pay off in good hard cash. With all our fine words, the barbarians know they're being taken for a sleighride and they don't like it. They live better than they ever did before, but we clean up. See?"

"Well . . ." This viewpoint was new to Teraf.

"Athena and General Ares are the only two people here (except me, maybe) who have the right idea," Hermes continued belligerently. "They want to pull in the outposts until we have consolidated our position in Atlantis itself and bring reinforcements from home, even if we have to kidnap them. But would Zeus give up a single colony? He would like . . ." He choked, glanced at his timepiece and jumped to his feet, apparently cold sober.

"Great Land of Nod," he cried. "I've only an hour to catch the last edition. See you later, Prin—Prince." The journalist dashed for the door, then turned back to add sheepishly:

"That nectar must have been potent. I have no business talking like this about the powers that be . . . especially to one of them. Consider my extreme depravity and forget about it, will you? But keep your eyes and ears open tonight."

And with that repetition of the Pitar's advice he was gone.

Chapter 2

Where today roll the blue waters of the Mediterranean there must once have been great areas of land, and land with a very agreeable climate. This was probably the case during the last Glacial Age and we do not know how near it was to our times when the change occurred that brought back the ocean waters into the Mediterranean. . . . The people of the Mediterranean race may have gone far toward the beginnings of settlement and civilization in that great lost Mediterranean valley. H. G. WELLS, *Outline of History*.

Teraf threw himself on a pile of cushions when the reporter had departed, deciding to catch a few hours' sleep before the conclave, which, he remembered, was an all-night affair. For a time he mulled over the things which Zeus and Hermes had told him but at last he sank into a slumber filled with comets and rebellious, pigtailed barbarians who tried to gore him with the ox horns on their helmets. He was awakened by the valet, who brought him the blue silk ceremonial robe which rulers of Atlantis wore on this momentous night.

The prince had an odd feeling of unreality as he entered the pillared reception hall, still adjusting the folds of his clumsy garment. The setting sun was casting long shadows through the western porticoes of the chamber, but, through the opposite windows poured the ghastly light of the comet. The two sets of shadows wrestled across the marble floors. This unpleasant sight must have been noticed by others for, at that moment, the palace lights were switched on. Their glow vanquished the shadows and brought back the world of every day.

Already the reception was under way. It resembled nothing else in the universe . . . except perhaps another reception planned by Pitaress Hera of Atlan.

The rulers of Atlantis—that is, members of the colonial court and the ten kings of the Mediterranean provinces and their entourages—were there, all clothed in blue. Guests in the openwork metal trappings of Mars, the short tunics of the Hellenes and Etruscans, the rough woolens of the Celts and the violently clashing dyed linens of the Egyptians were there also.

These latter had come to offer suggestions, present claims or make complaints at the conclave. Many appeared ill-at-ease in the splendor of the marble hall. Teraf, remembering the advice of Hermes, saw numerous barbarians casting covetous glances at the tapestries, the golden goblets and the jewels which adorned the robes of the women present.

After his years on the empty deserts of Mars, Teraf felt out of place in the crowded, noisy room. Outside it was not much better however. Food and drink were being lavished in the many dining rooms; the palace groves were melodious with orchestras and solitary musicians. Only in the outer reaches of the grounds was there comparative peace, and even here the comet-shine seemed an ever present menace.

Dr. Vanya finally located the prince and dragged him back to the hall where Zeus and Hera, seated upon twin golden thrones, now welcomed the multitude.

The Pitar's face was twisted with pain but he was obviously trying to play up to his wife. Hera, a short, blackhaired woman, once had been considered the greatest beauty of the countryside; but now, under the influence of good living and power, she had waxed somewhat heavy about the hips and mouth.

Holding the zig-zag scepter stiffly upright, his handsome face smiling down at his guests, the Pitar seemed a personification of power and kingliness. Occasionally he forgot his aching foot when his eyes happened to light upon the beauty of some barbarian girl.

Once again Teraf made the acquaintance of all that splendid hierarchy. And finally Hera beamed upon him as he knelt before the thrones and patted his hand in a motherly fashion when he stood up after the customary pledge of allegiance.

Athena, the Pitar's elder daughter, then slipped her arm through his and led him through the mazes of the palace while they talked of old times. Athena was a tall, finely-chiseled woman whose creamy red skin was set off startlingly by the premature whiteness of her hair. Teraf knew her well because, as secretary of colonies, she had always paid special attention to Hellas and had done more to civilize his native land by her gentle persuasion than all the school-teachers and soldiers provided by the Pitar.

"I want to have a serious talk with you, prince," she had said as soon as she met him; but thereafter their conversation remained confined to reminiscences. Athena appeared ill-at-ease and hesitant, as though she could not bring herself to broach the subject nearest her heart.

During their walk they met General Ares, a frustrated, quiet man whose gray eyes held a devil. Ares had little use for Alfhas and merely barked a greeting at Teraf before hurrying over to Hephaestus, the crippled engineer in charge of the power-broadcasting Tower of Bab El. The two were joined by Heracles, the hulking builder of the great dam which held the rising waters of the Atlantic out of the low-lying Mediterrancan basin. They then moved toward a portico and stood gesturing and pointing upward at the comet.

"Our long-tailed visitor seems to have got the old boys all stirred up," Teraf commented idly.

"That's what I've been wanting to talk to you about," began Athena. "I believe I can trust you . . ."

She was interrupted by a soft, throaty laugh. It came from Aphrodite, youngest daughter of the Pitar, who hurried up, jeweled hands outstretched to the prince.

"Oh Teraf," she exclaimed, prettily out of breath, "Father gave me a message to deliver to you alone. You'll excuse us, sis." She smiled rather condescendingly at Athena. "I'll return him in a few minutes."

With characteristic playful arrogance she carried him off to a quiet bower. Aphrodite, Teraf had to admit as he looked down at her bronzed oval face, was one of the most beautiful women he had ever seen on Earth or Mars. She was small but exquisitely formed, and she made the best of her charms by wearing a short blue robe which clasped with a pearl brooch on one shoulder and accentuated her rounded bosom and but slightly concealed the long line of her thighs.

It was of Aphrodite that the poets sang that she had been born of the sea foam. Yet, despite her allure, Teraf had the discourteous thought that, through years of keeping up her reputation as the court's queen of love, she was becoming a bit too voluptuous to merit that characterization.

"There is no message," she laughed when they were alone. "I just wanted to talk with you and I can't bear Athena any more. She thinks too much.

"Tell me about yourself since last I saw you," she rattled on as she drew him down on a bench decorated with carvings of the gods of ancient Atlan. "For years I've been dying to go home but father won't hear of it. He says there's too much work to be done here.

"But I hate it!" Suddenly her green eyes gleamed at him like those of a cat. "I dream of the courts of Minos and the other fair cities of Mars which I have never seen. Instead, I have to put up with these filthy Earthlings and the heat and the work . . . work . . . work. No one has time to play . . . with me." The last words were a whisper and an invitation. Almost with astonishment he found he was holding her in his arms and kissing away her tears.

At last he took her soft little hand and told of Mars as she liked to believe it was. He failed to mention the icy nights; the thin, piercing air which cut like a razor into the lungs of an Alfha; the horrors of the ever-encroaching deserts and the struggle for existence which made life on Earth a paradise by comparison.

She listened, almost purring with enjoyment. But, although his heart fluttered under the gaze of those great, glowing eyes, Teraf could not resist an inward grin at the memory of how he had painted the same beautiful picture of Earth for a bored Martian girl only six weeks before.

Their tete-a-tete was interrupted by a fanfare of trumpets from the hall. They hurried inside just as the crowd parted to admit a tall, blackhaired man in the traveling tunic of a Hellene.

Leaving Aphrodite with a word of apology, Teraf hurried

forward to greet his elder brother, King Refo. The latter saw him coming and halted in the center of the hall. They gripped hands.

"Sorry I couldn't meet you when you arrived," said Refo, the warmth of his dark eyes belying his almost expressionless face, "but great things are brewing in Athens. I'll talk of that later, but now I suppose I must pay my respects to His Ineffable Magnificence. Let's get it over with."

Arm in arm the brothers, so oddly different in type, approached the Pitar's throne. Refo was tall and gave the effect of blackness, like a thunderstorm in the distance. His aquiline face permitted no advances. His Martian father had given nothing to his son except the brilliant mind of a dreamer.

On the other hand, Teraf was pure Martian to all outward appearance . . . burnished hair, copper skin, extreme height, almost abnormally wide shoulders and the carriage of a wire-walker. But his happy-go-lucky nature was a gift from the gay little Achaean shepherdess who had bewitched his father when the latter was sent by Poseidon to colonize Hellas.

Zeus greeted the newcomer without the warmth which Teraf had expected. Both men merely bowed with fingertips to forehead and exchanged a few formal phrases. Teraf felt a chill over the room, and behind his back he knew the guests were whispering.

The tension was broken by another fanfare announcing the arrival of Plu Toh Ra, Pharaoh of the Egyptian province, with his daughter and heir, Pan Doh Ra.

Teraf drew in his breath sharply at the appearance of this couple. Plu Toh Ra was a veritable giant, all of seven feet tall and proportionately broad. His hawk-like face and hypnotic eyes gave an impression of ruthless strength. His features were fine, though the effect was somewhat spoiled by the fact that the bones of his face were clearly visible beneath the swarthy skin. His slanted eyes, black as midnight, wandered slowly over the crowd and Teraf noticed that there were few who could meet that glance.

The prince remembered strange tales of the power which the Pharaoh held over his millions of subjects. No Martian nor Alfha he! The Egyptian boasted that his ancestry traced back to Ra, the sun god himself, and that he paid fealty to the Martians only so long as he benefited thereby.

Educated on Mars after his father had bowed to the inevitable during the first years of the Martian conquest, the Pharaoh had returned unchanged to build up an empire within an empire. It was even whispered that he dreamed of some day being the first barbarian Pitar of Atlantis.

Tearing his eyes away from that dominant figure in its sweeping, violently-colored linen robes, Teraf turned them on the daughter. The difference between the two was startling. The Hellene vaguely recalled that Plu Toh Ra had married a Martian girl, but he was not prepared for what he saw. Pan Doh Ra, aptly named "A gift from all the gods" was slim and lithe, like a young panther, and her garment was, in fact, fashioned out of a panther's skin. Her eyes were twin pools of darkness which contrasted strangely with her hair, which was a sort of golden-black. Yet this intensity of coloring did not make her resemble in the slightest her cloudburst of a father.

She was, Teraf decided, merely a playful panther kitten, bewildered by being led through some thunderous procession. She should have been sunning herself by some cool stream. What would she become under the domination of such a father? He shivered.

Teraf and his brother still were standing before the dais when the Egyptians were escorted forward. The former thought he saw a quick glance of understanding pass between the two older men.

"Greetings, Pitar," said the Egyptian. "You seem worn by the cares of your high office tonight."

"Greetings, Pharaoh," was the equally sardonic reply. "Take care, or your own high office may become a bit wearing also."

The king of Hellas then introduced Plu Toh Ra to his brother and concluded the ceremony by leading the girl to the foot of the twin thrones.

"This, oh Pitar, is my betrothed, the Princess of Sais," he said proudly while Pan Doh Ra blushed.

"Not bad. Not bad," purred Zeus and then tried not to jump as Hera pinched him. "We give you our Pitaric blessing."

As Refo led the girl away while the crowd cheered, Pan Doh Ra smiled up at Teraf. Rather, it seemed, she grimaced pitifully. *Poor panther kitten,* he found himself thinking and then wondered why such a silly idea should cross his mind.

Chapter 3

. . . the people were gathered together every fifth and every sixth year alternately, thus giving equal honour to the odd and the even number. And when they were gathered together they consulted about public affairs and enquired if any one had transgressed in anything, and passed judgment on him accordingly, and . . . when darkness came on and the fire about the sacrifice was cool, all of them put on most beautiful azure robes, and, sitting on the ground, at night, near the embers of the sacrifices over which they had sworn, and extinguishing all the fire about the temple, they received and gave judgment. . . . PLATO's *Critias*.

The arrival of the Egyptians brought the reception to an end and marked the beginning of ceremonies incident to the conclave proper. Amid a blare of music, Zeus limped from his throne, entered a sedan chair and took his place at the head of a procession formed by members of his court, the ten kings and their resplendent retinues. The little column was followed by the sacred white bull which was to be sacrificed on the altars of the ancient Titan deities, Gaea and Uranus, in the sacred grove of the Gaeic Oracle.

Tradition had it that this was the thousand and second such procession to the shrine. According to old stories, Gaea and Uranus were founders of the race of Titans which had ruled Atlantis before the coming of the Martians. Even now, original inhabitants of the Mediterranean basin were known as Titans and still boasted of their high ancestry.

The invaders from the red planet, realizing the grip of the old sun and earth worship, had not endeavored to stamp it out; rather they had made use of its festivals and customs for their own purposes. Thus, although the old rituals were retained, the conclave—which had once been a purely religious gathering of the ten independent kings of Atlantis—now had become a conference of governors, where problems of trade, education, etc., were discussed.

The oracle of Gaea, a cleft in the floor of a deep cave through which issued gas that, in the old time, was supposed to make the priestesses see visions and issue cryptic advice, had been closed by order of the Martians, who felt it to be a menace to their regime. A high iron fence had been built around the cave and no one was allowed to enter, even during the conclave.

To the rhythm of devotional music played by both old fashioned stringed instruments and hidden loudspeakers, the procession moved slowly out of the hall and up the mountain. Ignoring the cable cars which connected the palace with Bab El, the participants walked in pairs, flanked by torchbearers. The two lines of dancing lights usually could be seen in all parts of the city and were the signal for public prayers. On this occasion, however, the effect was spoiled by the light of the comet, which cast its sickly glow over the landscape and made the torchlight impotent.

Teraf walked beside his brother, who had slipped a blue robe over his travel-stained clothing. Just behind them were the Egyptians. Although the other kings were surrounded by many advisers, the two Hellenes were unattended, as were the Pharaoh and his daughter. This was explained by the fact that the others had arrived in Atlan many days before, to take advanvantage of the city's hospitality.

The king of Hellas was in a bad humor. At first he walked in silence. Then, as the way became steeper and the procession lengthened, he burst forth angrily: "It's a shame. This is but a shell of our old religion. The red men are mocking us. In the old days, the free kings of Atlantis came here to worship their Gods. Now we puppets come to discuss tin imports from Britain."

"And in the old days those hungry, skin-clad kings parted to start new wars against each other," Teraf could not help interposing.

"Have your years away from home made a weakling of you?" snapped Refo. "Of course those old kings made war. War is the highest form of human activity. It tempers the will of the people. They lived hard and died gloriously. That was the Golden Age. Now even their oracle is defiled."

"Aye," boomed the mellow voice of the Egyptian from behind them. "Refo is right. Today we build factories, till the soil, fly through the air and . . . get fat. But some day the Celts, who despise us, will sweep over this land like a swarm of locusts! Hmmm!" His cadaverous face split in a smile. "Not a bad phrase, that: Like a swarm of locusts."

"But the Martians have a superior culture," Teraf protested. "They have advanced Terran culture a thousand years since they came, and neither Celts nor Titans can stand against their weapons."

"There speaks the Alfha," sneered the Egyptian. "A true

Titan would be planning ways to re-establish his kingdom. Why, one bold stroke could wreck the Tower of Bab El, cripple all their motive power, and . . ."

He felt the amazed eyes of the younger Hellene upon him and stopped short.

"We may count on you, Teraf, if trouble comes?" Refo burst out anxiously when the silence had become strained. "You'll support any struggle for liberty, won't you?"

"Say, what is this?" snapped the prince. "You may count on me to back Zeus to the limit. Brother or no brother, I advise you to say or do nothing further. As for you, Egyptian, crawl back into your mummy case."

Plu Toh Ra's yellow teeth showed in a bleak smile for an instant. Then he dropped back beside his daughter and, without another word they resumed the long climb. A quarter of an hour later they arrived at the valley of the oracle, a circular glade high up on Crooked Mountain and open to the view of the city beneath.

Great fires were lighted on the Altars of Heaven and Earth. The bull was slaughtered with many incantations by several priests in long white robes. (Teraf remembered having seen several of those same priests working as gardeners about the palace in a more prosaic garb.) Then the carcass of the animal was quartered and hung above the fires to roast. Until the barbecue would be finished, Zeus, ten members of his own court, and the ten kings sat on the ground in a semi-circle and talked about matters of state.

Since Refo occupied the seat allotted to Hellas, Teraf wandered into the forest, trying to arrange in his mind the many things he had learned since his arrival. It began to look to him as if the long rest he had earned during his years of furious study on Mars would not be forthcoming.

All about him, minor officials of the governing classes were building bonfires near which they would dice or play cards until the rising sun put an end to the conclave, and the carcass of the bull would be cut down and distributed for a morning feast before the return to Olympus Palace.

Heedless of where he was going, Teraf stumbled on. Hermes' warning; the coldness between his brother and the Pitar; the strange glance of understanding which had passed between Refo and the Egyptian, and lastly, the cryptic words which had passed while they were climbing the mountain all seemed to merit careful thought.

At one turning he came across the fence which barred entrance to the cave of the oracle. He skirted its sinister bars and turned at last to rejoin one of the groups seated about the friendly little fires which blinked in the distance. But he had taken only a few steps when he leaped backward, his heart pounding and his hands scrabbling at the entangling blue robe in search of sword hilt or heat pistol.

Before him, limned in the shadows, was crouching a nightmare. A five-foot-long, horse-like head armed with a double row of teeth, and surmounted by a tall horn or crest was darting at him on its thin, leathery neck. The thing had the body and wings of a bat, a thousand times enlarged.

Pterodactyl! flashed through Teraf's mind as he managed to get his dress sword free. *I'm done for!*

But the creature made no move toward him, though it rustled folded, parchment-like wings in an ecstasy of fury and made a sound like the hiss of escaping steam. Teraf was tempted to run, but his curiosity finally got the better of him. He approached carefully, to discover that the flying reptile was fettered with chains which hobbled its feet and passed over its wings.

He had completely circled the pterodactyl—first of the vanishing breed that he had ever seen alive—when a soft voice spoke at his elbow: "Don't be annoying Sonny. He never could abide strangers."

Teraf whirled, sword still in hand, to find Pan Doh Ra smiling at him out of the shadows.

"Is—is that delirium tremens yours?" he gasped.

"Certainly." The girl came forward and caressed the gibbering creature's head as though it had been that of a favorite horse. The Pharaoh won't ride in an airplane unless it's absolutely necessary. Says they're effete. He prefers to fly on the back of one of his own birds."

"You mean you have more of these outlandish creatures?"

"Oh my yes. We have a whole flock of them at Sais. Of course Sonny is the fastest and strongest of the lot. Want to pet him? He's quite calm now, aren't you, Sonny?"

Teraf felt no call to caress the brute, yet he didn't want to show his aversion. Sheathing the silly sword, he stepped forward and ran his fingers over Sonny's bony head and around its mouse-like ears. The pterodactyl now seemed assured of the friendliness of its disturber and purred like a cat.

"I'm the only one who can manage him," the girl said proudly. "The Pharaoh was in a hurry to get here, so he took Sonny—and had to bring me along to take care of him."

"But why didn't you land at the palace dock, instead of 'way up here?"

She shrugged and silently continued patting the reptile.

"They'll not be wanting us at the conclave until dawn," Teraf made another try. "Let's build a fire here and talk."

"I shouldn't. The Pharaoh wouldn't like it." But she made no further complaint when he struck a light and made a bonfire.

For a while they stared at each other in awkward silence, until Teraf half regretted his impulse to become acquainted with this wild creature. Unconsciously she had dropped into the conventionalized sitting posture of the Egyptians, legs crossed and hands on knees—like a living sphinx, he thought.

Out of the corner of his eye he watched the graceful, repressed little figure crouched beside the blaze in her outlandish short skirt and breastcloth of panther hide. She did not seem anxious to talk—seemed almost to have forgotten him and to be seated on a lotus leaf in contemplation. Pretty knees she had!

"I must congratulate you on your betrothal to my brother," he said formally, when he became conscious that his thoughts were leading him astray. "He's a splendid person."

She crossed her arms, placing one hand on each shoulder. (Another damned conventionalized attitude, the prince fumed.) Nice hands, though, with long, tapering fingers.

". . . a splendid person," he repeated in panic.

"Is he?" she asked simply. "It was the Pharaoh's wish." (This came as an afterthought.)

"Then you don't care for Refo?" He bristled slightly.

"Oh, he's all right—but he can't laugh." The answer was almost a sigh. Charming contralto voice she had.

"I didn't think you—your countrymen had much use for laughter."

"They don't. That's why I hate them so." There was a light in her eyes which was not a reflection from the fire. "But I learned to laugh in Minos . . . and I can't quite forget."

"You were educated on Mars!" Somehow the idea that this sphinx-faced beauty had not lived all her life among the pillars and pyramids of Sais came as a shock. But her statement awakened a bond of sympathy between them, and their conversation lost its strained character. They had mutual friends on the home planet. Both remembered the stark beauty of the deserts and the mad, gay battle for existence.

For an hour they chatted while Pan Doh Ra slowly lost her conventionalized manners and became just a laughing, carefree girl. Finally he told her of the oracle's cave and she expressed a burning desire to explore it. They succeeded in finding the gate at last, but it was locked and rusted fast as well.

Without a word, Pan Doh Ra ran back to Sonny, released the hobbles on his feet and brought him back on leash like a dog.

"Open it," she commanded, shaking the gate vigorously. The beast cocked its horned head thoughtfully, then hooked its skinny claws into the ironwork and surged back with a great flapping of wings. The lock snapped and they were inside.

"Good boy," crooned the princess, readjusting the hobbles as her pet nibbled a lump of sugar. "Let's go, and Gaea take the hindmost, as the Pharaoh would say."

They found a pile of half rotted torches inside the cave mouth and, lighting two of them, paced down the sandy floor between rows of stalagmites and stalactites which rose like curtains of silver and jewels on either side of the passage.

"I've heard the gas is dangerous," Teraf whispered, awed despite himself as the cavern opened like a cathedral before them.

"I stopped breathing long ago," his companion giggled in an attempt at nonchalance. "I'm scared stiff but I wouldn't admit it."

They tiptoed along through the whispering silence until a patch of light ahead caught their attention. It was a hole in the cliff wall through which the comet-shine streamed. In the floor of the cave was a corresponding fissure and from it issued a gray thread of gas.

"Let's just sniff it," she suggested as they approached through a double circle of rough hewn altars which encircled the oracle. "Maybe we'll see Gaea and Uranus themselves."

"Not on your life." Teraf gripped her arm.

But his precaution was useless; at that moment the volume of gas increased. It gushed from the chasm and filled the whole cave with vapors which eddied along the low ceiling like sheeted ghosts.

The Hellene started to drag the girl toward the entrance as a sweetish-acrid odor bit into his nostrils, but a lassitude seized him. His knees sagged and then he found himself lying on the sandy floor, with Pan Doh Ra beside him.

For a moment he was badly frightened; then a sense of well-being drove out the fear. At the same time the cave seemed to expand until it took in the universe. The beat of his heart assumed a slower and slower tempo until each throb was like the measured thud of a sledgehammer.

"How do you feel?" he asked the princess after he realized

that it would take them at least a thousand years to walk to the entrance of the cave.

"Lovely," she purred, stretching voluptuously. "Wanna stay here forever." To his hyper-sensitized mind the words came minutes apart.

For a time they were silent then. In the plane to which the gaseous drug had lifted them, centuries passed and generations were born and died. Then, in a calm, detached voice, Pan Doh Ra began talking as though at the prompting of an invisible psychiatrist.

For a time she spoke of her repressed childhood among the priest-ridden people of the Nile; of religious processions and rituals which made up most of the life at court; of sweaty caravans returning across the deserts from far places such as Cathay; of the aching sunlight and the choking duststorms.

As she talked, pictures swam before Teraf's eyes, as though he actually were witnessing the scenes she described. The gray billows of gas took form and color so that he watched the passing of the snorting camels and helped the beak-nosed, impassive priests perform unnameable rites among their towering monoliths.

Then the princess told of her few happy years on Mars where, through pressure brought on the Pharaoh by Zeus, she had been sent to be educated. And again, across the back of the cave, colors ebbed and flowed, revealing the fairy skylines of Martian cities; gay school scenes; jaunts into red wastes which had been waterless for a million years; friends made; and the gradual unfolding of a girl's vivid personality.

Next came the return to Sais to the barbarous, oppressive yellow and black palace. Pan Doh Ra's hand clutched that of her companion tightly as she related how Plu Toh Ra, now completely under the domination of the Seraphist priesthood, had crushed her back into the old routines.

She was allowed but one recreation and that only because she was a master at it. She trained the serpent-birds—last of their breed—which the Egyptians had half-domesticated ages before. They were kept in a den under the palace, ready for use as terrible engines of destruction.

Pan Doh Ra had a strange power over those nightmarish survivals. They would follow her like dogs, though with other persons—even those who occasionally rode on their backs—they were ferocious and intractable.

"I tamed Sonny myself," she boasted. "He's the largest and swiftest of the brood. But he had a devil. Still has. Once he killed three of his keepers in as many minutes."

She drooped and was silent for a long while, her wide eyes fixed on the column of gas bubbling from the floor. Teraf vaguely sensed her thoughts . . . her loneliness and misery floated like antic shapes across the mist.

"How did you meet my brother?" he ventured at last.

"Oh, the Pharaoh gave me to him as the price of Hellas' allegiance." Her voice had gone flat. "I know now that we're going to die here, so I might as well tell you everything."

"Gave you? Allegiance?"

"Of course. But Refo loves me as much as such a man can love any woman, I suppose. Last year he came to Sais on a visit of state and saw me. He begged the Pharaoh for my hand. Plu Toh Ra saw an opportunity to gain a powerful convert to his crusade. I was the price. He didn't have to do much persuading. Refo always longed to bring back what he calls the Golden Age."

"Then it's war?" whispered Teraf. "But that's ridiculous. In six months, half a million soldiers could be sent from Minos to Atlan."

"But in six weeks, Atlan may be but a memory if . . ." The girl threw out one slim arm to steady herself, then sank slowly to the floor.

With a desperate effort Teraf rallied his willpower. What had they been doing? Sitting there like two opium eaters. He managed to stagger to his feet, but to lift the girl was beyond his waning strength. He fell across her unconscious body, then, gripping her shoulders, tried to drag her away from the fissure.

He made some progress, but, as he crept past the leering Titan altars, his lungs drawing in great draughts of the gas, the cave seemed to expand until it reached the very stars, and the floor stretched endlessly before him. Finally he ceased his efforts and sank down to await the end.

Eons later he had a vision. A towering giant, its face covered with a white cloth, strode through the mists, taking one step every hundred years. Its voice boomed out like the tolling of a bell: "Great . . . Land . . . of Nod. Thought there . . . was . . . a . . . story . . . in . . . that . . . broken . . . gate. Hup there: Come . . . with . . . papa!"

Teraf's senses swayed into darkness.

Chapter 4

Which shaketh the earth out of her place and the pillars thereof tremble. *Job,* 8-6.

Teraf awoke in his room to meet the questioning eyes of little Dr. Vanya.

"What . . . ? How . . . ?" he stammered, sitting up quickly and then lying down just as suddenly when his head spun like a top.

Without a word, but with a look that spoke volumes, Vanya handed him a copy of the *Evening Planet.* Even stories of the comet's approach and of the conclave had been subordinated to a scarehead which read:

Planet Chronicler
Saves Prince & Princess.
Curse of Gaeic Oracle
Falls on Daring Pair.

Teraf read on until he learned that Pan Doh Ra had completely recovered from the effects of the gas but that his own case was "grave" before he tossed the sheet away.

Disregarding Vanya's pleas, he rose and dressed, feeling lightheaded still, but otherwise perfect master of himself. There was too much to be done for him to remain in bed. He could not doubt the meaning of Pan Doh Ra's last words. He thought of the Hellenes, always spoiling for a fight. They worshiped Refo and would follow him to destruction.

Then there was the possibility of a surprise attack by the Egyptians, with reinforcements for Atlan months away across 90,000,000 miles of space. He must tell Zeus, of course, but first he must find his brother and endeavor to dissuade him. And Pan Doh Ra? What of her, if Plu Toh Ra learned that she had disclosed the plot?

He must have been unconscious many hours for it was night again—as much night as it could be with the comet blazing overhead—when he stepped out into the palace gardens. For an hour he prowled the park, then turned back to the palace, his mind made up. He would try to make Refo see his error and, if that failed, denounce him before the court.

As he reached this point in his reasoning, he swung round a turn in the path and came upon a blackrobed figure, its arms uplifted, its face turned toward the comet.

"Oh, Uranus, God of the Skies, smite this proud nation that dares mock your rituals," words tumbled from back-drawn lips. "Return us to the Golden Age, when the din of machinery did not defile your sacred groves—when our youths were not debauched but followed in the footsteps of their fathers. Hurl your curse . . ."

"What mumbo-jumbo is this, Refo?" Teraf tried to make his tone casual although he was suddenly boiling with anger.

"You!" gasped the king. "I thought you were dying . . . that you would at least have the grace to die after bringing shame upon our house and that of Egypt. Get out of my sight, you false Titan."

"Have you been sniffling the oracle, too?" The younger man was flabbergasted. "What on Mars do you mean?"

"Mean? I mean that you have ruined the woman who was to have been my wife . . . that you . . ."

"*Was* to have been your wife?" Teraf's eyes narrowed.

"You heard me. The Pharaoh called me this morning, apologized for her disgraceful conduct and broke the engagement. She's being taken back to Sais now to become a vestal virgin, if her father can arrange the—ah—technical difficulty."

Teraf dropped his hand to his sword hilt, then gritted his teeth and made one more effort to talk to this madman. "If what you're implying actually took place," he choked, "would we have been found unconscious?"

"It would have been easy enough to hold your heads over the gas stream when you thought you were discovered." The king was beside himself with rage. "You're no brother of mine. Fawn on your Martians till God's blight falls on them, but never dare set foot in Athens again on pain of death."

"But you'll go back there to plot treachery against our father's people." The prince realized now that further pleas were useless. "I know about the revolt you're planning and by all the gods of Earth and Mars, I won't let Hellas be ruined to please a beetle-worshipping Egyptian."

"If you know that, then you must die at once." Refo whipped out his slender dress sword and lunged as he spoke. Half-expecting the attack as he was, Teraf leaped backward, escaped the thrust and jerked out his own blade.

They stamped back and forth across the wanly lit sward, each striving for an opening at throat or heart. The elder brother was the more powerful, but he was accustomed to swinging the two-edged Hellenic short sword, and had never had expert training with the nimble Martian rapier.

Step by step, Teraf forced him backward until he managed to hem him against the wall of an ornamental grotto where further retreat was impossible. Back and forth the thin blades quivered, always in contact. Twice Teraf drew blood from his opponent's breast, heart-high but not deep. Once he slipped on the dewy grass and felt an electric stab of pain as Refo's weapon grazed his side.

But the king was becoming winded. More and more wildly he parried the machine-like thrusts of his brother. His timing became inaccurate; his arms seemed weighted with lead. The time had come for the finishing stroke. Teraf's anger had been partially dissipated by the struggle. He knew his brother would never submit to disgrace. Should he kill him as an act of mercy? he pondered, easily parrying the tired man's blows.

As he pondered, the earth beneath them seemed to shiver, like a great beast awakening from sleep. The light changed subtly; shadows danced together about the grotto.

Refo, who had been facing the comet, dropped his guard and stared, the duel forgotten. Teraf turned and did likewise, while the ground heaved like the sea.

Against a background of ghastly green sky, the comet was growing! For several moments it gave the impression of rushing to engulf the Earth; but, as they watched in wonder, it split in two parts, then burst like an exploding shell.

The shock of that gargantuan explosion reached them a few breaths later. The earthquake redoubled, hurling them about like straws. A wind of hurricane proportions came howling at them from all directions.

For a moment Teraf lay face-upward on the trampled grass, staring stupidly at the remnants of the comet which were fading from sight like sparks up a chimney. Then a great tree which surmounted the grotto swayed and came crashing down upon him.

Chapter 5

A beautifully wooded park-like country surrounded the city. Scattered over a large area of this were the villa residences of the wealthier classes. To the West lay a range of mountains, from which the water supply of the city was drawn. Atlan itself was built on the slopes of a hill which rose from the plain about 5,000 feet. On the summit of this hill lay the emperor's palace and gardens, in the center of which welled up from the earth a never-ending stream of water, supplying first the palace and the fountains in the gardens, thence flowing in the four directions and falling in cascades into a canal or moat which encompassed the palace grounds and thus separated them from the city which lay below on every side. From this canal four channels led the water through four quarters of the city to cascades which in their turn supplied another encircling canal at a lower level. There were four such canals forming concentric circles, the outermost and lowest of which was still above the level of the plain. A fifth canal at this lowest level but on a rectangular plan, received the constantly flowing waters. *The Story of Atlantis*—W. SCOTT-ELLIOT.

Once more Teraf opened his eyes to stare into those of Dr. Vanya.

"Tut!" fumed the ancient. "Do you live at this pace all the time? I warn you, it will upset you. Twice in one day they bring you in here half dead . . ."

The prince pushed away those withered restraining hands and sat up. He was swathed in bandages and one shoulder ached infernally. "What happened?" he demanded. Then: "Where's Refo?"

"They said something about the comet exploding as the result of the opposing gravitations of Earth and Mars. Don't know much about it myself. Been too busy taking care of those injured by the earthquake to find out. Quite a few people killed. Tree fell on you. Dislocated one shoulder and caused a slight concussion. You'll have to stay in bed a few days."

"But my brother. What happened to him?"

"Sit down, young man! Calm yourself. Your brother is well. Carried you in here after the quake. Was bleeding from several contusions but wouldn't stay to have them dressed."

"Where did he go?"

"My dear boy, how should I know? Now that I think of it, he did tell me to say to you that he was sorry, though for what I don't know. Now try to get a little rest, like a good fellow."

But Teraf pushed him aside and stumbled toward the door. He must reach the Pitar before it was too late. The attack would come at once, he felt, since Refo must realize that the plot was known. He ran down the hall toward the audience chamber while the doctor trailed behind, protesting querulously.

The palace was in disorder. Here and there great cracks yawned in the walls, while chunks of marble and plaster fallen from the ceiling made going difficult. But workmen already were clearing away the debris while officials dashed back and forth through the rubble.

The prince found Zeus calmly dictating to Apollo various directions for rescue work in the city. He started up when the bandaged apparition entered, then waved away his gaping secretary and limped forward.

Teraf stammered out his story, half expecting to be disbelieved, but there was no doubt on the Pitar's face. Hardly was the tale told when Zeus, his lame foot forgotten, leaped to the television screen which filled one corner of the room. There he began pushing buttons and issuing crisp orders as directors of the various military stations appeared for a moment on the ground glass panel.

In the midst of this commotion the screen flashed imperatively and the hunchbacked figure of Hephaestus, seated in his office atop the Crooked Mountain, wavered into focus.

"Beg to report the city in flames in the fifth circle," he cried. "Looting has started in the warehouses." The twisted face faded and was replaced by that of Ares, whose pale gray eyes were blazing with something akin to joy.

"The City's in revolt," he chortled. "Have ordered out the first and second cohorts. We're holding most of the bridges, but the barbarians have captured several of them. Orders?"

"Throw up the fire screens," answered the Pitar. "After they're going, drop soldiers by airship where the police are hardest pressed. Are the barbarians well armed? Who's leading them?"

"Commander at Station Three reports Plu Toh Ra and Refo have been seen among the barbarians. Many of the latter are unarmed, and there seems no concerted plan of attack. This evidently had been planned months in advance, but was forced prematurely. Titans are taking no part in the attack so far."

The screen went blank. Zeus, walking as quickly as though he had two good feet, led Teraf to the window through which only a day before they had looked at the comet. It commanded a superb view of the city, with its five canals lying like concentric silver rings among the soaring buildings.

Many fires now could be seen blazing throughout the town. Through them little groups of Martians and Titans fled hither and thither, pursued by the barbarian hordes.

The second circle—that which enclosed the barracks—was, however, a bustle of organized activity. The relatively few soldiers were under arms and standing in solid ranks beside the airship hangars. Covers were being dragged from the infra-heat reflectors so the guns might be trained upon the principal avenues of approach to the citadel.

The greatest congestion was at the heads of the many canal bridges. At such points the attack seemed to be advancing in an organized manner and the loyal patrols were hard-pressed.

Then, as they watched, the water of the four inner canals caught fire! At first it boiled, then burst into flames as though it had been gasoline. These flames mounted, throwing clouds of inky smoke which hung low over the water. In their terrific heat many bridges melted and crumbled, dropping those who had been caught on them into the cauldrons beneath.

"There you have the horrors of war, prince," sighed the Pitar as he tugged vexedly at his curly beard. "Good, silly, brave men dumped to their deaths like rats. General Ares' diabolic invention is saving Atlan. For years he's been spending a large part of the military appropriation on chemical bombs which he sunk at intervals in the bottom of the canals, where they could be ignited by radio waves from Bab El. Doesn't last long. Look!"

Already the circular sheets of flames were dying and their smoke screens being swept away by the breeze. But what a different scene was presented as the air cleared. The barbarians now were stampeding, trapped by the canals which still were full of boiling water.

Now from the second circle, cigar-shaped, wingless airships were scudding over the city to alight on rooftops or public squares. As they touched ground, their quotas of fifty soldiers would hurl themselves upon some still belligerent group of barbarians. The police also were rallying, and the fire department had been working all through the melee extinguishing burning buildings.

"What's that?" Teraf gripped the arm of his chief and pointed as, from the fourth, or business circle, a tiny ship flashed upward toward the setting sun.

"White and gold, the colors of Hellas," gritted the Pitar as he leaped from the vision screen. "He must be stopped."

But it was too late; before the orders could be issued, the fast flier had disappeared toward the northeast. A moment later a mammoth bat-like thing soared up from the roof of one of the larger warehouses.

"It's a pterodactyl," shouted Teraf, who was sweeping the city with the Pitar's powerful binoculars. "It's Sonny!" He could clearly make out the chalk-white face of Pan Doh Ra and the now smiling countenance of her father as they were revealed by the reptile's flapping wings.

For a while it was touch and go. The pterodactyl was much slower than the ships which rose in pursuit, but it had a head start. And Sonny headed straight for the cloud of smoke which had been whipped from the burning canals and disappeared within it.

"They've escaped, too," sighed Zeus as he turned off the useless screen and limped wearily back to the window. "That smoke won't dissipate until nightfall. That means more bloodshed—more misery.

"I'm too easy, Teraf," he continued as he sank into his throne. "I've distrusted both Plu Toh Ra and Refo for months. Reports have filtered in—but I didn't believe it. What have they to gain? Liberty?" He laughed bitterly. "The barbarians have more liberty under Martian rule than any of them could have dreamed of a century ago. We have brought them release from their bickering, ignorant kings. We have seen that they no longer starve in the midst of plenty. By Chronus, we've almost made them our equals. And yet, for a bit of loot, they would still follow their old leaders. I don't understand." He unstoppered a flagon of nectar and poured a bumper of the heady liquor for his guest and another for himself. "Call Apollo," he groaned. "I've got to have this damned foot massaged."

Outside, in the lurid glow of sunset, the city was being restored to order. Fires were dying down; lights flicked on. A few leaders of the barbarians who had not been killed or arrested were urging their followers into suicidal attempts to break the cordons thrown about them; but their guns were exhausted, and their swords were pitifully useless against the ruby sparkle of the weapons of the soldiers and police.

To all appearances Atlan was returning to normal. And yet Teraf, studying the city over the top of his untasted glass, knew somehow that it would never be the same again.

Chapter 6

In the first place, they dug out of the earth whatever was to be found there, mineral as well as metal, and that which is now only a name and was then something more than a name, orichalcum, was dug out of the earth . . . PLATO's *Critias.*

His stiffened arm in a sling, but otherwise his old self again, Teraf reported to the Pitar the next morning. He found that most of the earthquake damage to the palace already had been repaired and through the window of the audience chamber he saw crews of engineers engaged in throwing temporary bridges across the canals. Otherwise there were few traces of yesterday's revolution on the gleaming capital.

Zeus had aged greatly during the night but his voice boomed with confidence as he greeted the prince.

"You did Atlan and Mars an unforgettable service," he said as he limped forward and slipped an arm around the other's shoulders. "As a reward you are to be crowned king of Hellas."

"But . . . Refo?" stammered the prince.

"He has been told to abdicate. Two weeks have been given him to come in and surrender. If he does not appear, it will be your job, I'm sorry to say, to go to Athens and bring him.

"Sit down," he continued. "The council is meeting here in a few minutes and I want you to hear what goes on."

Ares, the dour warlord, was first to appear, resplendent in new "campaign harness." Then came Hephaestus, looking like a kindly old vulture. Next Heracles ambled in turning his shoulders slightly to get through the door. Athena brought up the rear, accompanied by Hermes and Hera.

Zeus brought the meeting to order by rapping with his scepter.

"First," he said, "I want to explain why I asked the chronicler of the *Planet* to be present at this meeting. He has a habit of unearthing information which should be kept secret." He met the reporter's laughing eyes. "Hermes, I don't want anything published about what you hear discussed. Understood?"

Hermes sighed and put away his recording machine.

"Very well, then. There are three things to report. First, I have requested Minos to send us reinforcement. The reply has come back that three ships, carrying 15,000 troops, will be dispatched immediately. They should be here next month.

"Second—and this is highly important—a quantity of orichalcum has disappeared from the Bab El power station, according to a report just turned in by Hephaestus. What this may mean, you all know. Orichalcum is the highly radioactive metal which provides us with our motive power, charges our weapons and makes communication with Mars possible. The quantity missing is sufficient to blow Atlan to fragments."

"But that's impossible," gasped Hermes. "Only persons bearing the Pitaric seal are allowed to enter the storage vaults at the tower."

"Exactly!" The Pitar tugged at his beard. "That means only

one thing. There is a traitor in the palace. Every effort is being made to track him down."

Automatically the chronicler half rose from his chair, en route to the nearest vision screen with this scoop. He relaxed when Zeus rapped sharply with his scepter.

"The third matter before the council is a report on yesterday's uprising, the steps taken to prevent its recurrence, and the attitude of the ten kingdoms. Ares will discuss the first two points and Athena the latter."

"Beg to report," snapped the minister of war, as he lunged to his feet and hitched at his uncomfortable new trappings, "city quiet. Five thousand revolutionists killed. Twelve thousand wounded. Five hundred minor leaders arrested. Hundred twenty-three soldiers and loyal civilians killed. Wounded one thousand. Morale of army perfect, though munitions low." He looked down his beaked nose at the Pitar. "Temporary bridges will be completed by tomorrow."

Athena, her fine face drawn by a sleepless night, rose in his stead. The morning sun lit her soft white hair like an aureole about a face that was beautiful in spite of its high cheek bones, widely spaced eyes and almost abnormally high forehead.

"The colonies, with the exception of Egypt and Hellas, are faithful to Atlan," she said softly. "Due to the fact that the loyal kingdom of Arabia lies between the two seceding territories, there seems little chance of the latter joining in an effective attack.

"Refo does not, I'm sure, realize what he's doing. He is completely under the domination of the Pharaoh, who has played upon the Hellenes's imagination until he thinks he is a demigod sent to re-establish the old religions and lead the Titans back to a Golden Age which, alas, never existed. He needs disciplining."

"He'll be disciplined all right," grunted Zeus. "Prince Teraf will be crowned king of Hellas two weeks from today." Seeing an agonized look on Hermes' face, he added with a grin, "All right, boy. That's one story you *can* break, but stick around until the meeting's over. Continue, Athena."

"Plu Toh Ra, unlike Refo, is entirely evil," his daughter went on gravely. "He has listened too long to whispers by the priests of Sais. He has also become a little mad, I think, and should be killed. Refo is his tool and Pan Doh Ra his unwilling captive. The daughter is a Martian at heart, however, and is beloved by her people. She would make an excellent ruler of Egypt."

"I always said," beamed Hera as she laid her knitting in her ample lap, "that Pan was a sweet girl. Why I remember once when . . ."

"Hera, Hera," groaned the Pitar. "Can't you let Athena finish."

"Well of all things! I was just . . ." For once the Pitaress subsided, clicking her needles viciously.

"As for the outlying colonies of Africa, Asia and the Western Hemisphere," the secretary resumed, "all is quiet in those places at present. I would not, however, recommend the recall of any troops from the colonies, now that we are being reinforced from Mars."

She sat down and the Pitar looked at the others present, but all remained silent.

"I need more information," he grumbled at last. "This theft of orichalcum worries me. Hermes, here, is reputed to be able to make a sphinx talk. I intend to ask the editor of the *Planet* to release him to me for secret service work. Teraf is just back from Mars and should be able to notice things which we overlook as a matter of course. I think he should work with Hermes."

"Don't you think we should declare martial law?" Heracles' voice boomed out like thunder and made them all jump.

Ares nodded vigorously, but Zeus shook his head.

"The barbarians are but scantily equipped with infra-heat guns," the latter explained patiently. "Their air forces are negligible, being mainly merchant ships without arms. Hephaestus has disconnected the light beam from Bab El to Hellas and Egypt, so that neither of the seceding states can operate any machinery using radio power. That should cause the revolutionists to capitulate within a short time without the inconvenience of martial law. . . . Any other suggestions? . . . If not, the meeting is adjourned."

Chapter 7

. . . and there were many temples built and dedicated to many gods; also gardens and places of exercise, some for men, and some set apart for horses in both of the two islands formed by the zones; and in the center of the larger of the two there was a race-course of a stadium in width and in length allowed to extend all around the island, for horses to race in. PLATO's *Critias*.

Teraf spent the next two weeks wandering about the streets of Atlan, his face stained brown and his flaming hair covered by an Arabian burnoose. In his youth he had made many trips into that land to purchase blooded horses and, as a result, he knew the language and traditions of the inhabitants fairly well.

Due to the fact that Arabia lay between the seceding kingdoms, he represented himself as trembling in the balance between allegiance to Atlan and to the Egyptians, and was able to gather some information of value.

He found that most of the Titans—original inhabitants of the Mediterranean basin—were fairly well satisfied with Martian rule. The younger generation, which had been largely trained in Martian schools, considered itself a part of the ruling class and were working heart and soul for its preservation. But their elders, though they took advantage of every advance in civilization provided by their conquerors, talked of the good old days—which nobody really remembered. They muttered about the disrespect with which the Martians looked upon nature worship—although they themselves seldom entered the temples—and looked upon the burst comet as a sign of ill omen. Evidently a long propaganda campaign had been conducted among them by Plu Toh Ra's agents to undermine their confidence in the government.

It was among the new barbarian population, which had been brought in to meet the demands for labor created by the constantly expanding empire, that revolt stalked red-eyed and defiant. Although cowed by the ease with which their "oppressors" had won the first skirmish, Teraf could see that those hordes of half-civilized warlocks from western and northern Europe were merely biding their time.

The prince spent part of his time investigating the tower of Bab El, seeking some clue to the orichalcum theft. The power station fascinated him as of old. Its atomic pile and throbbing machinery seemed the very heart and soul of Atlantis. Its antennas pumped electric power into the ether as gas is forced into a balloon. Properly attuned receiving apparatus could tap this power at designated spots all over Earth, precisely as one might prick a balloon with a pin and withdraw a stream of gas.

The system had the disadvantage of being vulnerable to aerial attack, but it had been found extremely useful in a loosely knit empire, where colonies were often cut off from the mother country by stormy seas, deserts or savage tribes. Yet, except for disciplinary reasons, they could not be cut off from the boundless supply of radio power; and with it could operate their air freight and passenger ships and be in constant communication with Atlan.

This power was generated from orichalcum in lead-lined vaults underlying the 800 foot tower. It was in these vaults that Hephaestus brooded like a genie, hobbling about the gloomy passageways, darting into rooms which purred with shining machinery and quarreling ferociously and constantly with his staff, who loved him.

"Isn't she a beauty," the engineer crooned one day when Teraf came upon him caressing a transmitter as though it had been a woman. "A million kilowatts capacity. Enough to turn half the wheels on Mars itself. And Earth uses only a paltry half million kilowatts."

He escorted the prince into a great vault where the orichalcum was stored in hardened lead containers, each of which weighed a hundred pounds.

"It just couldn't be done," he muttered. "No one could carry out one of those shells under our very noses. He would have needed a truck."

"Couldn't the thief have drilled a hole through one of the containers and extracted the contents?" ventured Teraf.

"And get a mortal radiation burn doing so." The cripple scratched his hump nervously. "Oh, it could be done, of course, if one were fool enough. Let's look."

A careful examination of the chamber convinced them that Teraf's guess had been correct. A heap of lead shavings was found on the floor, and one container was pierced by a tiny hole.

"Some utter idiot did it," fumed the little engineer. "Carried the stuff off in a thin lead container which could give him practically no protection. He's dead by this time. Damn him, he should be, robbing us when we're so short of atomic fuel."

Teraf hurried to the palace with his news and ran into Hermes, who had made another important discovery. The latter believed he had the password used by the revolting Titans and their barbarian allies for the secret meetings they were known to be holding.

" 'Scrolling' is the word," declared Hermes. "It means some sort of particularly smelly savage and is the worst insult possible. Twice this week I've socked barbs on the jaw when they used the term on me. Saw the light today when one Norseman called another a Scrolling. Instead of battering each other to pulp, they thereupon shook hands and went arm in arm to the nearest saloon."

"Seems almost too simple," grumbled Zeus when he had heard their reports. "Hephaestus isn't accustomed to hiring utter idiots at Bab El, in the first place. As for the password," he tugged thoughtfully at his beard, "I don't trust it."

"But it's worth trying!" Hermes was boiling. "We can't just sit here and wait for . . ."

"I know. I know. Go down into town and try it out. But take the prince along, just in case you run into trouble."

So it was that, a few hours later, Teraf found himself seated on a stone bench at the race track which was the pride of Atlan and the marvel of her barbarian inhabitants. They could not understand the science of the Martians, but they certainly appreciated their wonderful horseflesh.

Here the immigrant workers, most of whom lived in the many "Strangers' Homes" which abounded in the city, congregated on holidays and after work. One of these outlanders, evidently a Norseman, sat beside the Hellene now. The latter picked his teeth with a long knife while he surveyed the racing with lackluster eyes and made derogatory remarks about the horses and their jockeys.

"Yes, we have much better horses in Arabia, my native land," Teraf agreed with his neighbor.

"Horses interest me little," yawned the Norseman, tossing his long braids of dirty yellow hair back over his shoulders. "Boats are my choice. And if yon cursed red men had not swooped upon me from the skies when my galley was peaceably raiding the British coast, I would be at sea now instead of watching this lousy show."

About them the crowd was on its feet, yelling as some favorite came down the stretch, but the barbarian scarcely designed to glance at the track.

"Definitely second rate," agreed Teraf, despite the fact that he had won a hundred credits on the race. "You say you once raided Britain. Tell me . . ."

Under his prodding, the barbarian waxed loquacious. He boasted of wild pirating expeditions along the northern coasts, of battles where the decks ran with blood, of the women he had stolen and the men he had slaughtered.

"And now," he mourned at last, "I become a mere trader in furs and tin because the red men have found that I know the north countries. A purchasing agent, they call me. Bah!" He spat on a lizard which had crept from under the grandstand to sun itself.

"But don't you have more gold in your pockets than in the old days?"

"Gold! I haven't seen a piece of good yellow gold since I reached Atlan. Instead they give me little pieces of paper for my hard work." He dragged a big handful of credits out of his baggy trousers and sneered at them. "Oh, for the wild times, when we could raid a Celtic town, fight from sunup to sundown, and come away with the holds of our ships crammed with real gold and the cabins with pretty, sobbing women. Then we could return to our fjords and live like kings for half a year."

"And wind up dead broke at the end of that time."

"Well, what of that?" The Norseman dug at his molars with the knife as if to uproot them. "Weren't there other cities? Now I have to fly about and chaffer with stinking traders whose goods I used to take without a by-your-leave. How they laugh at me. I tell you there's no future in this business."

"Why, when all is said and done, you're no better than a Scrolling," cried Teraf, heart in mouth.

The barbarian's face lighted up. He put away the knife and faced about. "You'll be at the meeting tonight?" he asked, tugging at one of his greasy braids.

"Why, uh, I've been out of town. I haven't received any notice of a meeting." Teraf wondered if *he* should have a braid to tug.

"It's at the old place—the East Catacombs," growled the Norseman as he rose to depart. "I'll see you there—brother." He walked away, treading with grim delight on the toes of other spectators.

Teraf and Hermes attended the meeting together that night, after the chronicler had disguised himself as best he could by swatching his great chest in a heavy woolen burnoose and staining his face brown. They had a general idea of where they were going, for the catacombs—or at least the entrances to them—were among the showplaces of Atlan.

These caverns were relics of a day long before the Martian invasion, when the capital had been a religious center known as "The City of Golden Gates" and built around the Gaeic Oracles. Monasteries had flourished there and the great of prehistoric Earth had been brought by thousands for burial in the sacred precincts.

It was into the only one of these caverns located on the eastern side of town that Hermes led the way. The entrance masqueraded as a grotto in a small park in the business circle. It was only after muttering their password through a tiny hole in a blank stone wall that a panel slid aside to reveal a flight of slippery, deeply rutted stone steps.

Feeling their way in the darkness, which was partially lit at long intervals by smoking torches, they came at last to the meeting place, a vast arched chamber, the walls of which were lined with crypts. Many of the latter had been rifled. From some protruded reminders of their contents—a grisly clutching hand, a grinning cranium or a shamelessly exposed thigh bone. The air was fetid and stifling, while the long shadows flung by the torches made the half-exposed skeletons dance a ghastly rigadoon.

The meeting evidently had been in progress for some time. A young man of decidedly Egyptian cast of countenance, but dressed in the leather shirt and baggy trousers of a Norseman, was haranguing 500 or so onlookers from a dust-covered altar in the center of the flag-paved floor. As the two spies entered, he was jeering at his audience's meek submission to the "red invaders" and painting a picture of revolt which drew yells of enthusiasm.

Yet, despite his eloquence, he spoke in generalities. There were no plans or names of leaders mentioned. The Egyptian seemed striving merely to arouse the blood lust of those present while keeping them in ignorance. At last he sat down amidst wild cheers and the clashing of swords. Such weapons, though their wearing had been forbidden since the first outbreak, were evident, nevertheless, in large numbers.

Teraf started and gripped Hermes' arm when the Egyptian was succeeded at the altar by his toothpicking Norse acquaintance. The hulking ex-pirate was still at it, though this time he was using an oversized splinter of wood. For several moments he leaned over the block of granite, letting his eyes roam casually over the gathering as though considering what he should say.

"I was afraid we wouldn't have a full meeting—after we changed the password so suddenly yesterday," he drawled at last. "However, I see you're all here. Also," he spat out the splinter, "I see we caught two Martian spies with the trick." His voice rose to a yell. "They're the ones by the door in Arabian costume. Grab 'em!" He leaped over the altar and charged, sword in hand.

The speaker's desire to work up a dramatic effect was what saved the intruders. Before the onlookers grasped the meaning of his words, Teraf and Hermes had elbowed their way through the outer ring of onlookers and were dashing down the corridor.

It was not the passage through which they had entered, however; that was shut off by several stalwart guards. But another passage ran off into utter darkness in an opposite direction and they chanced that one.

"One up for the revolutionists," laughed the reporter as they ran, stumbling over bones which littered the floor. "We'd better separate at the next intersection. That will throw them off and there are plenty of shafts leading to the surface which we can find when daylight comes."

They dashed on, bruising themselves against the tilted stone doors of the crypts, stepping on skulls which rolled and threw them sickeningly, panting in the vile dust which their footsteps stirred up.

Behind them the cry grew louder as their pursuers, snatching torches from the walls, picked up the trail. Soon the leaders of the pack were only twenty yards behind. A well-flung stone caught Teraf in the shoulder and spun him round, but he kept on.

The roar of shouts became deafening in the narrow tunnel. And to make things worse, several of their pursuers started an old wolf-hunting chant.

"We're done for—unless we strike a branch in the tunnel," gasped Hermes a few minutes later. "Their lights let them make better speed than we can."

As he spoke there came a high belling note close behind. It was the view halloa of a fleet-footed runner who had almost overtaken them.

Without breaking his stride, Teraf snatched a skull from an open crypt and hurled it with terrific force. The barbarian went down, his sword skittering along the floor almost within their reach.

Then, when their lungs seemed cracking, the passage branched. Without hesitation, Hermes took the right angle and Teraf the left. The pursuit hesitated at the intersection, giving them a moment of respite.

But the prince was exhausted; his legs moved like broken sticks and his lungs screamed for pure air. In the darkness he reeled against a wall and thrust out an arm for support. His hand plunged several feet among the bones and dust of a rifled tomb.

A way out flashed through his mind. Slowly he dragged his weary limbs over the edge of the niche as torches again began moving toward him. By their dim reflection he saw that the vault was occupied by an almost complete skeleton. He threw himself down behind it and rubbed the inch-thick dust over his burnoose in an effort to camouflage its stark whiteness.

"Sorry to disturb you, old man," he panted as he wriggled and turned to make himself as flat as possible. "There's a housing shortage, you know."

With a roar the pack approached, torches gleaming red in his eyes as he peered between a skull and shoulderblade, sword in hand for a last hopeless fight.

Without a glance at the crypt—one of the thousands housed in the tunnel—the barbarians swept by, their blood-lust up, their swords shaking above blond heads, their braids streaming so ridiculously behind them that Teraf had difficulty restraining a laugh.

Realizing far down the corridor that they had lost the trail, they began casting back and forth through the maze of tunnels for their victims. Teraf even made out that they started searching the crypts, but this soon was given up because of their great number. After that, the pursuers contented themselves with wandering back and forth for hours.

Once the fugitive thought he heard confused shouting in the distance, and trembled to think that Hermes had been taken. At another time the dust got into his nostrils and caused a violent fit of sneezing which almost led to his discovery.

But again the vast number of death cubicles saved him. After several hours the chase gradually died away until, by the time his watch showed that it was morning, the catacombs had regained their ancient stillness.

Cramped and stiff, he at last chanced creeping from his hiding place. Some whim made him try to rearrange the bones which he had disturbed, but they crumbled under his touch.

Then began a long, wearying search for the exit. He dared not return to the cavern where the meeting had taken place, and wandered for hours in the darkness. Dust got into his parched throat and choked him; bones and fallen stones tripped him frequently.

It must have been towards noon when he discerned light ahead. But when he reached it, he found that the tunnel had dipped and was blocked by a sheet of water, evidently part of one of the circular canals. Light was shining through this, however, indicating that liberty could not be far away.

Taking a long breath, Teraf dived and swam until his lungs were bursting. At last he came up, fearful that his head would strike a ceiling of stone. But luck was with him; he just cleared the end of the tunnel to attain the air and sunshine of the outer world.

Dripping like a half-drowned rat, he crawled ashore and hurried through the amused crowds until he found an aerial taxi which carried him to the palace. Not stopping to change clothes, he dashed to the audience chamber to report the probable death of Hermes.

When he was admitted into the Pitaric presence it was to find the debonair chronicler, freshly tubbed and clothed, seated in his old attitude on the small of his back, feet cocked upon the window sill and glass in hand.

"Great Land of Nod," chorted Hermes as he leaped to his feet. "Now I won't have to get drunk to commemorate your demise. Where *have* you been?"

"Don't be so flip," growled the Hellene. "I come in here all broken up to report your death and what do I find you doing . . . ?"

"Having a drink to drown my sorrow over *your* death. What's wrong about that? Let's have another to celebrate our return from the dead."

"Come, come, boys," snapped Zeus. "What happened to you, Teraf?"

Shamefacedly the prince explained.

"Did the same thing myself," chuckled Hermes, "but I had sense enough to sneak out the passage on the heels of the last of our charming playfellows. Well, it will make a better story for the *Planet* that there has been a relief expedition searching for *you* for hours. Didn't you hear us shouting? Heracles, who is in charge, finally ordered me back to the palace for a rest."

"Well, in that case . . ." Teraf found his anger melting.

"And I didn't get a single name," wailed the reporter as he refilled his glass and sank back into his chair. "That's one time when the *Planet* failed to get a scoop."

Chapter 8

Saw the heavens fill with commerce, argosies of magic sails; Pilots of the purple twilight, dropping down with costly bales.
Heard the heavens fill with shouting, and there rained a ghastly dew
From the nations' airy navies grappling in the central blue . . .
TENNYSON'S *Locksley Hall.*

Coronation Day for the new king of Hellas approached with no sign of a change of heart by Refo. The outlawed ruler even mocked at messengers sent from Atlan with demands for his abdication. They were returned under military escort with many presents, and bearing advice to Zeus as to the best method of conducting a sortie into the wild Greek mountains.

Plu Toh Ra did not bother to return messengers sent with a similar message to Sais. He sent back only their ears.

Meanwhile both sides in the struggle marked time. The Martians waited for the promised reinforcements while Hellenes and Egyptians contented themselves with border raids, calculated to excite their warriors with a taste of loot. General Ares fumed and fretted about those raids but had sense enough not to advocate weakening the defenses of Atlan by trying to stop them.

The coronation was being planned by Hera, who was determinded to make the affair so impressive that it would awe the barbarians into submission. The streets of Atlan were draped in bunting and banners. The serving staff at the palace had been augmented. Dr. Vanya, in his role of high priest, had ordered new robes, while his assistants ceased from their labors in the gardens and practiced rituals or incantations by the hour. And because Refo showed no sign of surrendering the ancient jade crown of Hellas, artisans and engravers of the court were busy creating an even more impressive diadem for his successor.

Teraf surveyed the creation in the shop of a palace lapidary with mingled emotions. He felt honored by the confidence which Zeus had in him, but, at the same time, felt that somehow he was betraying his brother. He forgot the fanatic he had met upon his return from Mars and remembered, instead, the boy—only three years older than himself—with whom he had played among the blue mountains of Thessaly.

He saw again in memory the day when, while hunting, they had been attacked by a saber-tooth tiger and he had stepped into a crevice in the rocks and broken his ankle. He watched Refo, black hair flying in the mountain window, standing across his body and defying the slavering beast with a puny sword in one hand and what appeared to be an equally impotent heat pistol in the other.

As the saber-tooth sprang, Refo had fired. Touched on the forehead by the scarlet beam, the tiger crashed upon them and died, covering both of them with its blood.

Those and other things, some humorous, some heroic, Teraf remembered as he stared down at the priceless crown.

"Put it away," he said coldly to the astonished lapidary.

Again the white palaces blazed with lights. Again the aristocracy of Atlantis moved through the spacious halls as on the night of Teraf's return. But whereas that ceremony had begun with gaiety, there was a sense of strain, almost of furtiveness, about the coronation, despite the efforts of the musicians and a plentiful supply of nectar.

The barbarians were conspicuous by their absence. Only natives of Atlan were present on this occasion, when, for the first time since the invasion, one king was to be degraded and another raised to his place. True, there was laughter and dancing. The cool skins of the women and the trappings of the men shone as brilliantly as before. But the Martians and the Alfhas regarded each other with a faint tinge of uncertainty, and Zeus cast few appraising glances at pretty girls.

In his chambers, Teraf was being prepared for the great occasion. His curly red hair was oiled and drawn tightly about his head with a silver band. He was obliged to don the long flowing robes of state and the clumsy, thick-soled buskins which had been worn by Hellenic kings since they first hewed their way from their Aryan birthplace.

The prince was puffing nervously on a last cigarette before making his entrance into the reception hall when the door swung open, and Hermes thrust himself through the attendants to survey his friend with sardonic humor.

"I'll bet you had more fun hiding behind that skeleton." He grinned, seated himself on the arm of a chair, and reached for the inevitable glass. "Want to talk to you alone a moment. I have a hot tip."

As Teraf waved the attendants away, the reporter snapped: "Where has Aphrodite been these last two weeks?"

"How should I know?" was Teraf's surprised reply. "I haven't seen her since the night of the conclave. Hadn't thought about her since."

"Don't let her hear you say that," chuckled Hermes. Then, in a more serious tone, "She has been 'lost' since the conclave —the night of the orichalcum's disappearance, if you recall. Sent word from Crete that she was taking the baths there. (She needs them, poor girl, at the rate she's going.) But I checked with our correspondent at Knossos. She *was* in Crete all right, but left ten days ago. And today she returns here to the palace, looking more done up than usual. How do you figure it?"

"Good Chronus, man! You don't suspect Aphrodite of taking the orichalcum?"

"Well, she has access to the Pitaric seal. And you know her

power over men, especially young ones. Don't forget there are plenty of young engineers at Bab El."

"But what could be her purpose? It sounds crazy to me."

At that moment the vision screen clicked imperatively and Vanya announced that the coronation ceremonies were about to begin.

"We'll talk some more about this later," said Hermes as he hopped to his feet and patted Teraf on the back. "Meanwhile, be a good king."

The ceremony was as impressive as the Martians—who secretly despised such occasions—could contrive to make it. Brave music played. Changing, varicolored lights wove a net of mystery over the silent, crowded hall. To a blare of trumpets Teraf padded in, flanked on all sides by chanting, censer-swinging priests in flowing garments of white and gold.

Approaching the throne, the prince knelt clumsily with the assistance of two of his escorts and received the Pitaric blessing.

Then Zeus rose and, bending forward, rapped Teraf on the shoulder with his zig zag scepter. Through some electrical hocus pocus, the thing flashed with blinding colors at the contact.

"Rise, King of Hellas," cried the Pitar in a great voice which shook the hangings on the walls, "and receive your crown at the hands of Vanya, high priest of Gaea and Uranus."

Hampered by the buskins, Teraf rose with as much dignity as possible and bowed his head for the weight of the crown. A querulous doctor no longer, but the minion of a power in which he still subconsciously believed, Vanya stepped forward supporting with difficulty that poem in green stone.

Hardly had he taken three steps when a terrific concussion shook the palace. The entire company in the audience chamber was hurled to the floor. A column collapsed, bringing with it a shower of marble which killed or maimed many of the panic-stricken guests.

Vanya fought to retain his footing; but despite his frantic efforts the jade crown flew from his hands and burst into a thousand sparkling fragments about Teraf's feet. Then the lights blinked out.

"An earthquake!" shouted some.

"The barbarians attack!" screamed others.

"Bab El is burning. Bab El is on fire!" a man who stood near the windows roared above the clamor.

Teraf fought his way through that mass of mad, squirming

humanity and reached a door. Staring upward in disbelief he saw the great steel tower of Bab El blazing as though it had been made of pine. As he watched, the tower bent slowly as if about to collapse. There, like a falling tree, it hung over the side as the impossible glow about it subsided.

After long minutes the palace lights flickered on dimly while the heat reflectors from the military section began to sweep the sky, although with only a fraction of their usual brilliance.

Teraf, and others who had managed to fight their way into the open, stared stunned at what the reflectors revealed—a great flight of monstrous birds circling over the city. From them were dropping bombs which set fire to anything they touched, even the marble of warehouses and palaces.

"Pterodactyls! The Egyptians are upon us!" shrieked the throng as it dashed about aimlessly. "Flee for your lives. Atlan is destroyed."

But another flight of "birds" was rising slowly from the military circles. This one was composed of the smaller fighting ships of Atlan. Apparently enough power still was being radiated by Bab El to lift them into the air. But they moved slowly, their anti-grav motors working sluggishly.

Even in their crippled condition, however, they were more than a match for the pterodactyls, which were capable of carrying but one man against the airships' ten or fifteen. Realizing their disadvantage, the riders of the winged reptiles wheeled their mounts low over the palaces, dropped the last of their bombs, and swept into the night with a thunder of leathery wings.

Here and there a gun would flash from one of the closely-pursuing ships and a pterodactyl, with an ear-splitting squeal, would fold its wings and drop like a stone.

Then, as complete victory seemed in the grasp of the Martians, the tower atop the crooked mountain reeled on its melting supports and collapsed with a roar.

Teraf watched the ships with fascination. For a time they hovered uncertainly. A few made quick landings from low altitudes. But those high in the air were not so fortunate; as the power drained from the ether they started falling—slowly at first, the luminous paint of their hulls making lurid trails against the sky, then with terrific speed they plunged downward, lighted from beneath by the burning city.

One struck on the lawn of the palace and burst like an egg, hurling maimed and dead occupants in all directions. Teraf covered his eyes and was sick as succeeding crashes told of the fate of most of Atlan's aerial navy.

Chapter 9

At the head of the Egyptian Delta, where the River Nile divides, there is a certain district which is called the district of Sais, and the great city of the district is also called Sais. PLATO's *Timaeus.*

Teraf was aroused from his stupor when someone shook him violently. It was Hermes, his face streaming with blood as he babbled insanely of scoops and extras.

"The vision screens aren't working," the chronicler screamed above the uproar, all his mocking *sang froid* forgotten. "I have to get to the office and write my story. But," he waved vaguely toward the mountain, "I saw one of those damned snakes fall over there. It seemed only crippled. Maybe you can catch the rider and get some information. Zeus said go after him. Gotta go now . . . write story minimizing damages and all that rot. Luck!" Hermes flung the last word over his shoulder as he started a staggering run down the path toward the nearest bridge.

His teeth gritted in fury, Teraf started a mad race up the mountainside. He too remembered having seen a giant shape flutter to the ground near the end of the garden.

In the dim glare of burning Atlan, the paths were unfamiliar. He stumbled through hedges, crashed into age-old trees and finally lost himself completely. Out of breath he halted and listened.

At first he heard nothing; then a faint sobbing reached him, apparently straight ahead. Thanking his star that the pocket gun he gripped was unaffected by the collapse of Bab El, he moved stealthily forward. Either the pterodactyl's rider or an Atlantean was badly hurt somewhere nearby.

The moaning stopped and he cast about for several minutes without success. Then it began again behind a hedge only a few yards from where he crouched. Teraf pushed through the foliage and came upon a dead flying reptile, its wings outstretched in broken folds like the sails of a wrecked boat, its teeth bared in a fearful grin.

For a time he watched the carcass, fearful of an attack from behind it. Then he crept forward, as the sobbing stopped once more.

"You might as well surrender," he said firmly. "We have you surrounded. Where are you, Egyptian?"

"Here," gasped a voice almost at his feet. "My leg is broken. I cannot harm you."

Feeling about in the dewy grass, Teraf located the body of the rider and, after much pulling and hauling, succeeded in drawing it clear of the dead beast. Then he lifted the wounded soldier in his arms.

"Kill me now and be merciful," groaned his captive.

"Oh shut up!" he commanded. "Zeus wants to see you."

The figure in his arms shuddered with another attack of sobbing. "I don't want to see him. Please kill me. I couldn't bear to have the Pitar look at me."

Unheeding the pleas, Teraf tramped back toward the palace. There great fires had been lighted to aid rescue workers. One of the palaces was in flames; several sections of the gardens blazed unchecked, but most of that last consignment of bombs had missed their marks.

As he entered the circle of firelight, where the barbaric uniform of his captive could be seen, Teraf was greeted with shouts of fury.

"An Egyptian!" screamed a dishevelled fury who but recently had been a sedate matron attending the coronation ceremonies. "An Egyptian dog!" She shook her fists wildly above her head. "Kill him! Kill! Kill!"

As Titans and even some Martians crowded forward to do her bidding. Zeus strode forward, his face black with anger, and his scepter spitting flame.

"By my immortal soul," thundered the Pitar. "If anyone lifts a hand, I'll strike him dead. King Teraf, put the prisoner down here by the fire. I want to question him."

None too gently, the prince placed his burden on the ground and stepped back. The Egyptian buried his face in the trampled grass and recommenced that heartbroken moaning.

"What's this?" Zeus dropped to his knees, his gout forgotten. "A mere boy. Turn over, son. Nobody's going to hurt you." Gripping the captive by the shoulders when no response was forthcoming, the Pitar lifted him so that his face was in the light.

The Pitar started back and Teraf caught his breath. Even the encircling crowd forgot its blood-lust and muttered in amazement. The flames revealed the clear-cut features of Pan Doh Ra, princess of Sais.

"By my thunderbolt," snorted the Pitar. "Pan Doh Ra! So you have betrayed us too. Carry her to my apartment, Teraf. I must talk with her alone."

In the battered royal suite, lighted now only by lanterns, the Hellene placed the girl on a divan and started to retire.

"Wait!" commanded Zeus. "Call Vanya to dress her wounds. Return with him." Then, turning to the suffering girl he sighed, "Has it come to this? Are my own people turning against me?"

"I had to do it," gasped Pan Doh Ra, sitting up and facing him squarely, though her face was drawn with pain. "You know the Pharaoh charged that Prince Teraf had disgraced me at the cave of the oracle. He swore he would place me among the vestal virgins of the goddess Neith. Oh Pitar, you can't imagine the hopeless, miserable lives those girls lead. Servants of the goddess they are called. Slaves of the priests they are in reality, sealed in a chamber of horrors too awful to mention."

"I know only too well. Continue, my child."

"I swore my innocence. I groveled at his feet and begged and pleaded. Finally he agreed that if I went along on this attack he would forgive me. I was to hearten the soldiers with my divine presence." She laughed bitterly.

"Those were orichalcum bombs, weren't they?" The Pitar shifted his attack. "Where did the Pharaoh get them?"

"Oh yes. Explosive bombs would have been too heavy for the 'dactyls to carry. The orichalcum was stolen from Bab El, according to the soldiers. Just how I don't know. I've been locked in my rooms since I returned to Sais."

"Then you know nothing of the Pharaoh's plans?"

"Only rumors. Others in the raiding party whispered that this attack was made to destroy Bab El and demoralize you. Plu Toh Ra, curse him for an unnatural father, is brewing some greater devilment in collaboration with Refo of Hellas.

At this point, Teraf returned with the priest-physician and the girl's examination began. She bore it bravely, although perspiration stood out on her face and she bit her lips until they were smeared with crimson.

"No broken bones," the doctor grunted at last. "Bad strain of all muscles in the left leg. She should be up and about in a few days. Numerous contusions and cuts. Wonder she's not dead. Perhaps I should say a pity." And Vanya took his morose departure, leaving the three together.

Zeus limped to his chair and sat down with a tired groan. For a long time he stared out over the burning city, then said softly: "Are you really with us or against us, princess?"

"With you," she cried, "to the last drop of my blood. What

do you want me to do to serve Atlan? I'll die willingly. How can I best help?"

"By going back to your father at Sais," replied the Pitar.

"But you can't ask her to do that," protested Teraf. "Plu Toh Ra might kill her."

"More probably he'll kill *you,*" replied Zeus somberly. "You're going to head Pan Doh Ra's escort.

"Now wait a moment." He held up his hand as the girl protested in her turn. "Unless I'm mistaken, the Pharaoh has at least one soft spot in his black heart—that reserved for his only daughter. Oh, I know that his sister, Medea, has great influence over him, but I doubt that he has any fondness for such a witch. He will be glad to have the princess brought back, though he may pretend differently. He can't decently kill her escort. But . . ." the Pitar's eyes narrowed, ". . . her escort may just possibly succeed in killing the Pharaoh and putting an end to this ridiculous war."

"But, sir!" Teraf was flabbergasted. "What could such a few men do in the heart of Sais?"

"Plenty—perhaps—with the secret weapons which Hephaestus can supply. And if they are imprisoned, some may escape and bring back valuable information—about the orichalcum, for example. I know it's a long chance, Teraf, but you are a bright lad. We'll discuss it further at the Council meeting in the morning."

Chapter 10

Zeus, the god of gods, who rules with law, and is able to see into such things, perceiving that an honorable race was in a woeful plight, and wanting to inflict punishment on them, that they might be chastened and improve, collected all the gods into his most holy habitation, which being placed in the center of the world, beholds all created things. And when he had called them together he spake as follows: PLATO's *Timaeus.*

"The news is bad," said the Pitar the next morning, after Hephaestus, Heracles, Ares, Athena, Apollo, Hera, Hermes, Teraf, and, last of all Aphrodite, had taken seats about the pillared Council Chamber. "Hermes, the minutes of this meeting must not be published. First of all, listen to this report from the spacer *Barthia.*" He spread out a purple heliogram on the table before him.

" 'Spacer *Manthus* lost with all hands approximately 45,000-000 miles out from Mars. Ran into uncharted band of extremely large meteors, a residue of the comet which recently exploded. *Manthus* riddled and drifted sunward. Apparently all on board suffocated when hull punctured.' "

Zeus lifted a tired hand to still the babble, and continued:

" 'Spacers *Barthia* and *Sonus,* running ten and twenty thousand miles astern of *Manthus,* pulled up in time to escape with slight damages. After intensive scouting, beg to report that spacelanes between Earth and Mars completely blocked by mass of meteoric material lying in plane of ecliptic. Standing by for orders.' "

"I have something to report on that," interrupted Hephaestus. "The observatory checked on the meteor band as soon as the helio was received. They say the meteor band has established an unstable orbit—if you can call it that—midway between Earth and Mars. The orbit is expanding slowly, however, due to the fact that the comet was traveling faster than the sun's planetary system when it burst. This should mean, they say, that eventually the meteor band will stabilize its orbit somewhere between those of Mars and Jupiter. They can't estimate how long that will take . . . or what will happen to Mars when its orbit coincides with that of the meteors."

"Thank you, Hephaestus." The Pitar spread out another heliograph. "Here's one dated from Minos and signed by the secretary of the Anarchiate. It reads: 'Due to reports from spacers *Barthia* and *Sonus,* have ordered both return Minos immediately. No hope of salvaging *Manthus.* Doing all possible to find path to you. Courage.'

"You know what that means," the old man said calmly as he removed his reading glasses and swung them between finger and thumb. "The 15,000 soldiers and the supply of orichalcum cannot reach us until a way has been found to deflect the meteors or until they change their orbit. This may require years—even centuries. Or it may happen next week."

"But can't a ship be sent over or under the meteor band?" cried Athena.

"Unfortunately not. Our spaceships operate by means of the force of gravity between the sun and its planets, and therefore can move only in the plane of the solar system. That leaves the situation strictly up to us, my friends."

The councilors still sat stunned, with the exception of Aphrodite—who, Teraf observed, yawned prettily and inspected her long red fingernails in the corner to which she had withdrawn—and Hera, who was bursting with excitement.

"I told you so," cried the plump little woman. "I had a dream two months ago about whirling suns and water. Oh, if you'd only listened to me and thunderbolted a few barbarian leaders instead of making eyes at barbarian women! I warned you . . ."

"Be silent, woman!" thundered the usually meek Pitar. "This is no time for your nonsense. Hephaestus, what's the situation at Bab El?"

A look of blank astonishment on her plump face, Hera subsided. In her place the hunchback rose, gripping the back of his chair until veins stood out on his gnarled, burned hands.

"We have rigged a temporary tower through which power can be broadcast for the city of Atlan and its immediate environs," he whispered in a voice almost gone from a night spent in shouting directions to workmen up there on his mountain top. "The heliograph to Mars is working, as you know, but we haven't enough power to raise distant radio stations of the empire."

"Not bad. Not bad," beamed the Pitar. "Continue."

"It will take from six weeks to two months to repair the main tower. Until then the city can operate normally, but no airship communication can be maintained with the colonies due to lack of power."

Heracles waved a great paw and demanded: "Does that mean we're completely cut off from the ten nations around the Mediterranean Basin? I'd been planning to inspect my dam . . ." He looked hurt and puzzled, like a scolded child.

"You'll have to walk on those big feet of yours for once," piped up Aphrodite from her corner.

"Or perhaps you can find an internal combustion motor car in the museum," said Zeus. The Pitar smiled in spite of himself. "Proceed, Hephaestus."

"Bab El station itself suffered only slight damage. The orichalcum pile is intact. However, our supply of radioactive fuel can last only a few months. As you know, ninety per cent of it was imported from Mars. Our own pitchblende mines will not begin to supply the empire's demands."

He sat down amidst oppressive silence.

"And your report?" Zeus glanced at the fidgeting warlord.

"Army morale good," barked Ares. "City normal. Damage extensive but repairable. Can hold off any attack with present force. Pterodactyls negligible quantity since many killed in attack and we now prepared for surprise." He popped back into his seat.

"Athena, what have you to say?"

The tall secretary of colonies rose wearily, brushing the silver hair away from her high forehead.

"We're in radio communication with all parts of Atlantis proper," she began. "The eight loyal kingdoms are disorganized due to the power cut-off, but report they can carry on until Bab El is restored. Reports from Crete say that Egyptian and Hellenic raiding parties have crossed the Mediterranean Lake and are active in that vicinity." She hesitated and then added softly, "In other words, the lights are going out, but we are managing to re-light most of them—for a while, at least."

For a long time Zeus sat fingering his scepter and staring out over his beloved Atlan.

"Friends and councilors," he said at last, "we will still rekindle all the lights and save the empire. The barbarians must travel on foot, on horseback, or in extremely small numbers by pterodactyl. They have a few infra-heat guns, and apparently a supply of orichalcum with which to charge them and manufacture light bombs.

"We cannot underestimate their leadership in the light of past events, but they are in the minority. Ninety per cent of the Titans, which means almost every inhabitant of the valley with the exception of those in Egypt and Hellas, are with us—at least so long as we keep up a good front."

"As things stand," Ares agreed, "we can defend Atlan, but until Bab El is restored we can't get our ships into the air or make an attack of consequence."

"Right." The Pitar leaned forward tensely. "At present, the key to the whole situation lies at Sais, where Plu Toh Ra holds his supply of stolen orichalcum. Princess Pan Doh Ra was captured last night. I'm going to send her back under the escort of Prince—of King Teraf, and fifty of the best men in Atlan's garrison. That will put some of our men behind the enemy's lines."

"That sounds awful silly to me," yawned Aphrodite. "I'm sort of fond of Teraf and would hate to have to look at him without any ears—or maybe any head. What on earth do you expect to accomplish by such a stunt?"

"I'm glad to see you back in the Council Chamber, daughter," answered the Pitar sourly, "but perhaps you had better acquaint yourself with the situation before you begin making suggestions. I say it's worth the risk to get a few of our people into Sais. Some may be killed and some imprisoned, but I doubt that Teraf will be harmed. He may be able to pick up some valuable information. However, let's put it to a vote. All in favor of sending the King of Hellas to Egypt at the head of the escort, raise your hands."

Every hand but that of the spoiled darling of the court went up.

"Thank you," said the Pitar as he rose carefully to his feet. "Now will you all remain here for the audience which I have arranged with our people?"

Apollo leaped to the vision screen and turned dials and pushed levers. The oval clicked and glowed as Zeus strode forward regally.

"Titans," he thundered at the machine, "this is no time to mince words. Egypt and Hellas have seceded from the empire and by sneak attacks damaged Bab El and our city.

"But the brood of filthy reptiles on which they rode were dispersed or killed by our brave fliers, crippled though they were. The attack harmed us little, and the rest of Atlantis is untouched and rallying to our aid.

"When Bab El is repaired we shall sweep over Egypt and Hellas like a plague of locusts. Until that time, be of good courage and fear nothing. If you support Atlantis she will reward you as in the past. If you desert her, the Egyptians will reduce you to slavery. Your women and children will be butchered, as in times of old, and you will be slain or starve where now you live in plenty."

"I don't like that *if* stuff," Hermes whispered into Teraf's ear. "The old boy should be more positive."

As though he had heard the comment, Zeus lifted his scepter, threw back his leonine head and shouted: "All those who have faith in me, join in our Song of Empire."

Then, as the Council burst into the rousing, space-haunted chant, the white-haired ruler led his phantom audience.

"Listen," whispered Athena.

Through the open windows the song echoed back at them, rolling in like a swelling wave as a million inhabitants of Atlan, who had gathered before the street corner vision screens, joined in the refrain.

"The people are with us," the secretary of colonies murmured to Teraf. "Yesterday's raid, which killed hundreds of innocent bystanders, has enraged even the resident barbarians."

"Shall I tune off, sir?" inquired Apollo as the song ended and Zeus stepped away from the screen.

But as he spoke the oval was splashed with vicious colors which slowly coalesced into a face. Hera screamed as the features became clear, revealing the hawk-beaked, swarthy countenance of Plu Toh Ra.

"He's interfering on our wave length from the Sais station," gasped Apollo. "I'll turn off the power."

"No," yelled Zeus. "Let him speak. Otherwise the people would think we were afraid."

"Slaves of Atlan!" The Egyptian's voice rang high and clear. "Pharaoh Plu Toh Ra, your liberator, speaks! How long will you toil like oxen so that this alien empire may grow? How long will you tolerate these wizards from another world who defile your gods and mock your sacred customs? Why must we send tribute back to Mars? Remember, we people of Earth are entitled to all the fruits of Earth. And remember that a land without gods is accursed."

"Nuts!" interjected Hermes. "Get to the point, Pluto."

"This is my warning," the voice roared on. "Rise at once and destroy your Martian oppressors. Rise! Or we shall destroy them and you with them. Not a living thing shall escape me. Plu Toh Ra has spoken!"

As the screen went blank, Zeus stepped forward calmly.

"Titans! Barbarians! Martians!" he boomed. "You have heard the generous promises of one who calls himself your liberator. Which do you choose? Atlan or Egypt?"

Athena gripped Teraf's arm again. "That is our answer," she cried, her eyes shining with tears.

Once more through the windows came pouring the heart-stirring strains of the imperial hymn, louder and with more fervor than before.

Chapter 11

"'Skin me, Brer Fox,' sez Brer Rabbit, sezee, 'snatch out my eyeballs, t'ar out my years by de roots, en cut off my legs,' sezee, 'but do please, Brer Fox, don't fling me in dat brier-patch,' sezee." *Uncle Remus*. JOEL CHANDLER HARRIS.

Six days later Teraf stood before the Pitar receiving his last instructions. Beside him was the princess, able to walk again and well on the road to recovery.

"My boy," said the ruler kindly, "you are going on a mission from which you may not return. Nevertheless I feel it my duty to send you. Frankly, the situation is desperate so long as

Egypt retains possession of the orichalcum. I'm gambling you and fifty of my best men on the forlorn chance that you can get to that orichalcum and either escape with it or explode it. It's a suicide mission. You are free not to go if you prefer."

"I'll go."

"No," cried Pan Doh Ra. "It's hopeless. The whole party will be slaughtered."

"I'm not so sure." The Pitar pointed to three small flat packages on his desk. "Here are three weapons which I believe you can smuggle through the Egyptian lines. Dr. Vanya will explain their use to you before he seals them to your skin in such a way as to defy detection by anything except X-rays. If you use them well, I believe you can best the Pharaoh.

"The escort will be under the technical command of Captain Jason of the Pitaric guard, but final decisions will be up to you, Teraf. I'm sending Heracles along at his own request. He's spoiling for a fight and needs some action. Heracles is not too bright, but he can be depended on. You'll also have Theseus, one of my best men. I'm also sending Nestor. He's old, but he knows Egypt like the palm of his hand. Castor and Pollux are both good navigators, and . . ."

"Navigators?" puzzled the Hellene.

"Yes, since all our aircraft are grounded, I'm sending you on the *Argo*—you know, the sailing yacht I use for trips on the lake. It will take you right up the Nile to Sais." He fingered his beard. "That's about all except this: Princess, if Teraf fails, I shall depend on you to keep us informed of goings-on in Egypt."

"Of course," answered the girl, lifting her dark head proudly. "But I still think Teraf is too valuable a man to be sent on this mission. There's Hellas to consider, too."

"Is that all?" The Pitar frowned slightly.

"No it isn't!" She limped forward, leaned her small fists on the desk and looked the Pitar straight in the eye. "If you must know, I'm in love with that redhaired Hellene and I don't want to see him chewed by a pterodactyl or bitten by an asp!"

"Well," Zeus chuckled at Teraf's startled gasp, "I can see your point under those circumstances. But can you see mine: That the empire is bigger than the best of its citizens?"

For a moment longer the princess stared into those wise old eyes. Then she bowed gravely, fingertips to forehead. "The Pitar has spoken," she replied in the old Egyptian formula. "From now on it's up to me to keep Teraf in one piece. When do we start?"

"Now see here, young lady," stormed Teraf, coming out of the coma into which her astonishing series of declarations had thrown him. "I'm perfectly able to keep myself in one piece."

"You've not been to Egypt recently," she replied. "We have devised more unpleasant ways of killing people than any country on Earth."

"But I won't have you acting as if you owned me. Why, I scarcely know you, and you have the impudence to say . . ."

"Now, now, my boy, don't get excited," warned Zeus, who was thoroughly enjoying himself. "I had been worried about Pan this last year or so. Thought her father had bewitched her or something. But now she's acting like the kid who used to throw this palace into an uproar every time she came to Atlan . . . Remember, Pan, when you and Hermes set up that three-dimensional movie projector and sent the image of a sabertooth galloping right through the grand ballroom?"

"Will I ever forget it . . . or the spanking you gave me afterward."

"Hera made me do that. Spoiled one of her fanciest parties. My hand still hurts when I think of it. We were afraid for a while it might cause an intercolonial incident."

"Oh, for the sake of Chronus, stop it," groaned Teraf. "You two act as if I were a pawn in a chess game. Don't I have anything to say about my love life?"

"I'm afraid not," chuckled the Pitar. "If Pan says she wants you, she'll get you. . . . And I'm not so worried as I was before about your returning from Sais." His voice became suddenly grave. "Now run along to Vanya with these weapon packages before I become maudlin and keep both of you here, empire or no empire."

Teraf found the *Argo* to be a spanking little craft and its crew to be the toughest collection of daredevils he had met since he used to hang around the spaceport as a boy. Every one of them had played a big role in the development of Atlantis, and now they were raring to go on their new mission.

"Nothing to it," boasted the tall, slightly cockeyed Theseus as he paced the silver-inlaid bridge and thumped his mighty chest. "I helped whip the Mayas into line and, boy, they were plenty tough. Pluto, here we come."

"Pyramids! Pyramids and sphinxes! That's all the Egyptians know how to build," agreed Heracles. "Now my dam . . ."

Old Nestor injected a sour note as he caressed his long nose: "It won't be so easy," he muttered. "The priests of Sais know a lot of tricks. They've kept alive a lot of the psychological knowledge of old Lemuria."

"Magic," jeered handsome young Pollux, who had wandered up with his inseparable brother. "Magic is no match for Martian science."

"Maybe so. Maybe so." Nestor scratched his gray head. "But just the same, I was talking to a renegade Egyptian on the dock a while ago. He was dithering about what he called the clashing islands, which guard the harbor of Sais. And he said neither our radio nor our sails might work when we got into the Nile. I'm glad the *Argo* has a bank of oars. And I've brought along a crate of carrier pigeons, just in case we are cut off from Atlan."

"Worrying as usual, Nestor?" chuckled Jason as he signalled for the mooring lines to be cast off. "You needn't, so long as I'm in command."

The old man muttered something highly uncomplimentary and trudged off to feed his birds.

Accustomed as the Argonauts were to the lightning speeds of interplanetary and stratosphere travel, the snail-like pace of the yacht became irksome to the extreme after the first day out. Not only that, but the water was extremely rough and most of the intrepid crew soon found themselves green with seasickness. About the only persons on board who were not affected were Teraf and the princess.

The Hellene, still miffed by Pan Doh Ra's amorous avowal, at first tried to avoid her. But he had to admit that she was very easy to look at as she laughed and joked with members of the queasy crew. Apparently she had not a care in the world; but out of the corner of his eye he often caught her watching him with a deeply worried expression. At last he could stand it no longer.

"Why did you tell Zeus you loved me?" he demanded as he leaned against the swaying rail beside her and stared out across the water toward the blue mountains of distant Crete.

"Perhaps because I meant it. Perhaps to save your precious hide." She grinned impishly at him over a slim shoulder. "Let's forget it, anyway, and try to plan some way for you and the others to escape from prison."

"But why are you so sure we'll be imprisoned?" He tried not to notice what a pretty picture she made with her curly black hair flying in the breeze. "I'm betting that your father will load us down with gifts for bringing you home safely and then try to pack us out of the country before we have a chance to learn anything of value to Atlan."

She looked at him with lackluster eyes. "You've been away too long, Teraf. Egypt doesn't abide by the old customs any more. Give you free passage!" She snorted. "Privately I think Zeus must be in his dotage. If I didn't know you were a stubborn fool, I'd ask you to tell Jason to turn this boat around immediately."

"Look!" His voice was savage. "There was a girl at Minos who talked to me the way you do. I finally had to tan her hide for it."

"I can well imagine, you big brute." She cuddled up against him and giggled. "But I've been spanked by better men than you, and it didn't do any good. I'm immune. Now stop making love to me and listen . . ."

And she launched into a description of the prisons in Sais which made his skin crawl. Festering, lightless dungeons; diabolic torture chambers; callous jailers anxious to simplify their labors—all became much too real as she described them to the last detail.

"There's only one possible means of escape from the palace, once you're inside of it," she continued. "Our brood of pterodactyls is kept in the sunken palace courtyard next to the dungeons. According to a quaint old Egyptian custom, they must be fed on human flesh. Enough prisoners are kept always on hand to glut their appetites."

"But what's all this got to do with my escape?" Teraf was feeling slightly ill. "Must I arise like a phoenix after being devoured by those reptiles?"

"Well, for all practical purposes, yes. Here's my plan. When Plu Toh Ra finally announces your imminent departure from this life, display an awful terror of the 'dactyls. Beg him to kill you in any way but that. Get down and grovel on the floor, if necessary. It's an old trick, but I think it will work.

"Your pleas will so delight the Pharaoh that he will immediately consign you to the feeding pens. These are next to the den and divided from it only by heavy iron bars. Often one of the creatures will thrust its head through those bars, grip one of the prisoners before his time comes to die and—oh, I'm sorry." (Teraf was livid.) "There's a streak of Plu Toh Ra's sadism in me, I'm afraid. We'll talk no more about that."

She waited while the crew brought the *Argo* about on the other tack to the shouted orders of Castor and Pollux, then, when the booming sails had quieted, continued gravely.

"My idea is just this. All the 'dactyls will follow me like chickens. I've trained them for years and have that control over them—call it telepathy if you will—which good jockeys have over racehorses. I can even talk to them after a fashion —like this . . ." She set up a shrill keening through her firm little teeth. It was half musical, half discordant and somehow disturbing, even to Teraf.

"You see? Well, after you are placed in the feeding pens, I'll slip into your cell some night. I imagine one of those packages Vanya gave you contains some sort of jailbreaking device. So you'll cut the bars and I'll lead you to safety. Father will conclude that you have been eaten. If you are still lucky, you can make your escape to Atlan with at least some information."

"It sounds snakey to me," groaned Teraf, "but if you think I can't possibly escape from the prison proper, I suppose it's our best bet. Now please talk of Atlan, or Minos, or . . . the principles of interstellar travel . . . something as far removed from 'dactyls as possible."

It was early morning of the third day when the Argonauts sighted the two squat stone towers which guarded the narrow entrance to the river port of Sais. As they crept slowly toward shore they had plenty of time for misgivings as to the success of their mission. Suddenly the most intrepid of them realized that fifty men, even though equipped with guns which could melt everything in their paths, still were no match for an army of heaven knew how many thousand wild-eyed barbarians.

"I, for one, wish I were safely back in Atlan, sipping nectar in some tavern," Castor had the courage to mutter.

"Those clashing islands, now," mumbled old Nestor, who had at last recovered from a severe attack of sea-sickness. "What do you suppose they might be?"

"Maybe those ugly towers," Teraf mused. "Pan, do you know?"

"There's something about them," frowned the girl, "but it's a military secret. I'm not sure . . ."

Using the oars against the current because the breeze had died, they edged the boat forward.

"I have an idea—for once," boomed Heracles, his flat face expressing genuine astonishment at his own cleverness. "Let's send something ahead of us into the port and see what happens."

"What?" jeered Theseus, who respected the engineer's brawn but not his brain.

"How about Nestor's crate of carrier pigeons. It's about the only thing on board that isn't made of metal."

And so—to make a legend, though they did not realize it—

this was done after a makeshift sail had been rigged atop the box.

The sun had not yet risen. The great river and the harbor seemed asleep as the Argonauts rested on their oars and waited. Slowly the crate drifted toward the towers. When it was squarely between them, the massive pieces of masonry started to move. Slowly and silently they slid toward each other across the channel as though operating on well-oiled grooves. They met in mid-stream, crushed the box as delicately and completely as a fine trip-hammer can crack a walnut and started a leisurely retreat toward shore. One pigeon, minus its tail feathers, fluttered out of the wreckage.

"Pull, boys!" Teraf shouted to the goggling oarsmen. "I think we can get through before the towers get back into position and are ready to close again. Maybe we can get ashore unobserved. This devil's device will make the Egyptians careless."

The men put their backs into the work while Jason handled the wheel and Castor and Pollux trimmed sail. The *Argo* reached the downstream edge of the moving towers before they had returned to position. But it was only halfway through the channel when the juggernaut began its second murderous advance.

"Pull!" yelled Teraf. "Pull or we're all dead men."

The *Argo* leaped like a racehorse under the impulse of fifty pairs of straining arms, but the towers slid forward inexorably.

The Hellene shut his eyes after gripping Pan Doh Ra's hand tightly. Seconds later there was a rending crash and he commended both their souls to heaven. But, after that, nothing happened. He opened his eyes and stared stupidly at Jason, who was spinning the wheel aimlessly.

"The rudder," gulped the captain, staring over his shoulder at the solid barrier behind them. "The towers pinched it off as our stern slipped through."

Inside, the crowded port was still asleep in the sunrise. Not a soldier was in sight, so they grounded the crippled boat and stepped onto the nearest quay, a shivering and thoroughly scared company.

"Now what?" asked Teraf.

No one answered.

"Pan, have you any idea where that orichalcum might be cached?"

"Oh yes," she chuckled mirthlessly. "It's somewhere in the palace. Why? Are you planning to storm the place?"

The Hellene's quandary was solved by a most extraordinary phenomenon. At first it appeared that a whirling cloud of dust —one of those tiny funnel-shaped twisters which often sweep across the landscape in summer—was building itself up before him on the quay. But there was no wind and the water was calm as a mirror.

As they all stared, the outline of the cloud sharpened; its nucleus darkened. Then, in a flash, its diaphanous quality vanished as it assumed the form of one of the most beautiful women they had ever beheld.

She was divinely tall—all of six feet—with raven-black hair and eyes, finely-chiseled features and the bearing and garb of a goddess. Her piercing glance surveyed the Argonauts one by one and finally settled with approval upon Jason's robust physique.

"Our Brother, the Pharaoh," the newcomer spoke in a deep, resonant voice which somehow suggested the tolling of death bells, "bids us congratulate you on your clever escape from the clashing islands and requests that all of you—with the shameless exception of the former princess Pan Doh Ra—be his guests."

"But— But—" floundered Jason, his eyes big as saucers. Teraf could see that, despite his astonishment at her materialization, the susceptible captain had fallen in love at first sight and was cudgeling his none-too-sharp wits, for some gallant reply.

"Say you accept, idiot!" whispered the King. "And try to make love to her unless you want to be fed to the fish. It's our only chance now."

"We accept the Pharaoh's invitation with pleasure," gulped the poor fellow. "To whom do we owe such a generous welcome?" He wasn't doing too badly, now that he had started.

"Oh, that's my aunt Medea," snapped Pan Doh Ra, her face an icy mask. "She always turns up where she's least wanted."

"Quiet, brat!" The words dripped venom. Then, with a flash of her brilliant smile at Jason, "Yes, we are Medea. And we are most happy that you accept our invitation, even though it will deprive us of the pleasure of seeing you tortured. Follow us."

Considerably shaken by that last remark, the little company followed the princess through the awakening streets of that monstrous town, past avenues of stony-eyed sandstone sphinxes and vast temples which had taken the toil of tens of thousands of slaves to erect.

Teraf noted that the early rising townspeople seemed little

interested in their progress, only surveying them for a moment with dull eyes before continuing with their labors. Since the cutting off of radio power the city had returned to manual labor, and once he caught sight of a gang of slaves engaged in some sort of military construction.

"Your people take their loss of freedom calmly," he whispered to Pan.

"They never were free except when officials from Atlan visited Egypt," was her bitter reply. "They pretended to be happy when foreigners questioned them because they knew they would taste the whip later if they did otherwise."

They fell silent as Teraf cudgeled his brain to make it remember bits of gossip which had drifted into Atlan from the rival court at Sais. Medea, he recalled, was said to be a sorceress who knew as many of the secrets of ancient Lemuria as her cunning, half-mad brother. It was rumored that she dreamed of ruling Egypt, but that the rigid law of succession decreed that, in the event of Plu Toh Ra's death, the crown must go to her younger brother, Absyrtus and, after him, to Pan Doh Ra.

"And Medea knows how to turn old men into young ones, and vice versa, through some drug she possesses," spoke up Pan Doh Ra, who must have been following his thoughts. "If you don't believe this, look at Jason. Already she has him behaving like a bashful boy, instead of the heart-crusher he claims to be. You may see him wearing diapers tomorrow."

Further conversation was halted because, at this point, they reached the palace. They had made the trip from the quay without being challenged by a single guard or soldier. Plu Toh Ra seemed content in the power of his magic to protect himself and his sister.

The Argonauts trailed into that tall, dull red structure in sheepish silence, feeling themselves elbowed and overawed by the sphinxes and frowning, black-clad priests with which it abounded.

Jason went ahead with Medea, and Teraf was well content with this, even though he admitted that the witch had sinuous hips and shoulders that would make a sculptor weep for joy. They passed first through an incense-clouded temple, where other priests, clothed in white, swung censers and chanted monotonous anthems before shadowy altars. The place was alive with sacred cats, whose green eyes slitted from dark corners or from the tops of the altars themselves.

They all breathed more freely when they passed out of those oppressive precincts and entered the throne room. There the

Great Man—or was it the Great God?—lounged on his lion-headed chair, surrounded by lovely women, perfumed courtiers, and slaves waving ostrich feather fans. One of his jeweled hands stroked the ears of a huge yellow cat which purred huskily under the caresses. Both Pharaoh and cat surveyed the newcomers coldly as they halted at the entrance to the room.

"You will turn over all your weapons to us now," said Medea and waited serenely until all the thunderbolts had been collected by two shiny Nubians. Then she led them across the rectangular chamber paved with balata stones of violently clashing colors.

Teraf studied the ruler closely as they took the one hundred ceremonial steps to the throne. Plu Toh Ra, though still young, looked surprisingly like his own mummy. The dark skin was drawn tightly over the bones of his face until it shone like parchment, and splendid robes of state could not conceal the equal gauntness of his mighty frame. Yet this was emaciation without a trace of weakness. The Pharaoh resembled some engine of destruction from which every superfluous ounce of weight had been hewn away.

"Welcome, oh men of Mars," he said when the Argonauts were grouped before the dais. "We have awaited your coming with impatience. It is a pleasure to receive—ah—ambassadors from besieged Atlan, particularly when they return to us our precious daughter."

"Was that a crack?" mumbled Theseus, flexing his muscles until Teraf shushed him.

Then the Egyptian clapped his hands and, when Nubians appeared out of the shadows, commanded that food and drink be brought.

"Maybe it's poisoned," whispered Nestor as the visitors sat down before a sumptuous breakfast of milk, honey and strange fruits.

"Don't be a fool. He's playing with us, as his cat would with mice," Teraf answered between mouthfuls. "I'm pinning my hopes on Jason. Watch him work."

Truth to tell, if looks could do it, the captain was laying his scarred heart at Medea's feet and she was relishing the experience.

Plu Toh Ra waited in sardonic silence until his guests had appeased their appetites. Then he dismissed the slaves and turned abruptly to Teraf.

"So you had yourself named as escort for our daughter," the Egyptian sneered. "Not content with the opportunity you had in the Cave of the Oracle, I see." Suddenly pretending to recognize his daughter, who, until then, might have been the invisible woman, he roared: "To your quarters, harlot! Out of our sight."

Teraf's face went white. He took a long step forward as the yellow cat bristled to twice its size, and guards about the throne swung their spears toward his throat.

"Your Majesty jests," he choked. "Zeus Pilar has magnanimously returned your gallant daughter, who was wounded in the attack upon Atlan."

"So 'tis said. So 'tis said. 'Tis also whispered that her escort hopes to return and report upon the military strength and activities of Egypt."

Teraf said nothing, but his heart thundered. Was Hermes' wild speculation about Aphrodite correct? The Egyptian's thin lips spread into a grimace at his discomfiture.

"We regret to tell you, our altruistic benefactor, that all is fair in love and war. Ha!" He beckoned to a scribe who stood nearby, stylus and tablet in hand. "We have coined a phrase. 'All is fair in love and war.' Write that down for posterity, slave.

"No, my dear boy." He picked up the cat and stroked it thoughtfully. "We fear that you and your companions can never return to Atlan. Prison, and then, when the Martians have been exterminated and we have more time to be amused, the asp, a slow poison, or possibly the pterodactyls."

Teraf wondered whether this was his cue to grovel, but he did not move, even when soldiers, at a signal from the Pharaoh, stepped forward and gripped Pan Doh Ra by the arms.

"We see Heracles among you," the living skeleton rambled on. "It was very thoughtful of poor old Zeus to send him along. We need an engineer at Sais to tell us how to build a Bab El of our own."

"But I'm a *civil* engineer," rumbled the big fellow. "I don't know nothin' about electronics. I can build a bridge or a dam, but . . ."

"Too bad. You will have to learn, then, and with great rapidity." The Pharaoh's ivory teeth flashed. "For your friends will be allowed to live only if you provide us with radio power. Then your red-skinned fellows at Atlan will be given the choice of submitting to Egypt or being destroyed. Oh," he cried, his face lighting up with a frenzied ecstasy, "we know that you Martians claim Earth as your rightful heritage. We know that your ancestors fled to that planet when the ice mountains overwhelmed Lemuria. We know that Mars is becoming a desert now and that you are returning in haste to the world you deserted so basely.

"But do not forget." He rose from the throne, threw back his proud head and lifted clenched fists. "Do not forget that others who were not cowards remained on Earth and through millennia of hardship kept alive a portion of the knowledge of ancient days. They, not you, shall inherit Earth." He recovered his composure somewhat and turned again to Heracles.

"Your companions will be held as hostages while you teach us electronics. If you serve us well, you and they will receive high honor and office in Egypt—and in Atlan."

"And if I refuse?" Heracles, his good, stupid face paling, uncoiled to his full height of eight feet and slouched forward.

For answer, Plu Toh Ra clapped his hands. At the sound, linen curtains which covered the right hand wall of the chamber parted. From them stood forth at least 200 warriors, their armor flashing and swords unsheathed.

It was then that Teraf played his ace. Reaching inside his tunic, he ripped the first of Vanya's packages from his chest, tore it open with his teeth, and hurled its contents into the faces of the soldiers.

Instantly a pall of midnight blackness spread over their half of the chamber. Behind it the Egyptians could be heard screaming and coughing. Hephaestus' invention was doing its work well.

"Seize the Pharaoh," the Hellene shouted, realizing that the pall would last only a few moments.

The Argonauts turned to obey, but they were too late. The dais was vacant, except for the golden cat which licked its chops and grinned at them with more than animal intelligence.

"Make a break for it!" he yelled as soldiers began groping through the cloud. Then he darted down a corridor which opened on the opposite wall of the throne room with the other heroes pell mell on his heels.

Down one interminable hall after another they dashed, turning and twisting, while the sound of pursuit began pounding behind them. Again and again they crashed into locked doors, but always managed to find an open exit.

After a while they began to get worried, however. Their wild race wasn't leading them into the open, but rather into the bowels of the earth. Yet there could be no turning back. Their lead over the pursuit was decreasing rapidly.

At last, at the junction of two more corridors, Teraf thought he perceived a faint gleam of daylight to the left. "This way," he called, and dashed in that direction, only to collide with a crash against some obstruction not fifty paces farther on.

The blow partially dazed him but he staggered to his feet to discover that he was staring through a grating of heavy iron bars into a sunken courtyard. And in the center of that yard were fluttering a multitude of squealing pterodactyls!

He shook the bars but they did not budge. He stumbled along the barrier in search of a door. There was one, but it was locked. Desperately he ordered the others to return the way they had come. Before they could do so, the inner door to the chamber slammed shut with a clang and they heard the grating of heavy locks.

"You have fallen neatly into our trap, Men of Mars," the voice of the Pharaoh came faintly through the door. "We wait your decision—for one day!"

In that dark and noisome cellar Jason called the roll and found that everyone was present, although not a few were badly battered. As they were preparing to hold a council of war, a faint moaning attracted their attention. It came from the farthermost corner of the room, and seemed to issue from a bundle of rags. Turning this over Jason revealed the pale and haggard features of the once-proud Atlantean ambassador to Sais.

"For Chronus' sake, keep them off me!" the prisoner screamed when the light struck his eyes. "Ow! They'll tear me to pieces. Help!"

"Keep what off you?" Teraf reached down and shook the quaking ambassador until his teeth rattled. "Snap out of it. I'm Teraf of Hellas. The others are friends, here to help you."

The man partially recovered from his delirium and pointed a shaking hand toward the bars which formed one entire wall of the cell.

"The dragons," he whimpered. "They keep reaching for me. I'm going insane." Then he hid his face and burst into another fit of blubbering.

It was only then that the Argonauts turned their attention to the courtyard. What they saw made the hair stir on their heads and made them feel like blubbering too.

Creeping toward them was a line of the ghastliest creatures ever seen outside of an attack of delirium tremens. Teraf was somewhat prepared for the sight but the others were dumbfounded. Big, the creatures were, as horses, with scrawny necks all of ten feet long and wicked little triangular heads in which burned eyes as old and cruel as the fires of hell. They were stirring up clouds of dust by beating their leathery wings on the ground as they advanced. There must have been a hundred or more of the black devils. Soon all were chirping and hissing as they thrust snakelike necks between the bars and tried to grip the prisoners with their long yellow teeth. The Argonauts crowded back against the inside wall and stared silently at the nightmare brood.

"They feed prisoners to them," gabbled the ambassador. "I'm to die that way tomorrow unless I tell Plu Toh Ra how to generate power from his stolen orichalcum. And I don't know! Save me!" The former dandy and favorite of the court was reduced to tears once more.

"Shut up! Pull yourself together, man. We'll get you out of this," lied Teraf.

But how? He couldn't think of any possibility of escape. A check revealed no weapons but a few knives. Even if they could pick the lock on the cell door, guards must be swarming outside, ready to toss them to the reptiles.

As if to prove this latter theory correct, a door was opened on the other side of the courtyard and soldiers thrust two trembling wretches into the den. The 'dactyls half-flew, half-ran toward their breakfast. Awful screams rang out. The Argonauts turned their heads away and were sick.

That long day and the night which followed were grisly nightmares. They crouched against the dripping wall as far as possible from the grille, saying little but thinking much on their sins.

When dawn came at last, the corridor door creaked open, guards shoved a big jug of water into the cell and tossed hunks of sour bread on the floor. Then two of the soldiers gripped Teraf by the arms and dragged him back to the throne room where the Pharaoh and his cat were sitting as though they had never moved.

"You are clever, Hellene," the Egyptian began without preamble. "We have talked to our daughter." He nodded toward Pan Doh Ra, who had entered at that moment and was now pacing sedately across the balata pavement. "She feels that we have wronged you—that with a little, ah, conditioning, you might become a useful ally, like your brother. No. Do not answer yet. Take time to think it over. Because of this, we have arranged to remove you from the dungeon and give you quarters more worthy of your high estate."

Remembering his previous conversation with Pan Doh Ra, Teraf was panic stricken. He *had* to stay in the dungeon! In the emergency he did the first thing that came to mind—spat on the sacred cat, which had advanced from the throne and was fawning at his feet.

The results were electrical! The cat spat back at him and clawed his legs. Plu Toh Ra leaped to his feet, screaming with horror. And a trio of priests leaped forward to wipe the fur of their god.

"Blasphemer," gabbled the ruler when he found voice to do so. "To the pterodactyls with him! No!" as guards sprang forward, "something better than that—the poison called curare which comes from across the sea. We personally will . . ."

Sensing that his only chance was slipping away, Teraf fell flat on his face in a grovel.

"Oh, your gracious majesty," he cried, "I thank you for your mercy. I can face poison—anything, but not—not the pterodactyl den again. Spare me that. Remember that I did bring back your daughter. I call Chronus to witness that I did not harm her. Chop off my head! Burn me! Poison me! But don't, I pray you—don't throw me into the den."

For a moment he thought he had overdone it, but the the monarch swallowed the plea entire. Stepping from the throne, he prodded the Titan gingerly with the toe of his upturned sandal.

"So that's the way the wind blows? (Aha, slave, make a note of that pretty phrase.) Well, by my Ka, the 'dactyls are really not so bad as you think. Still, feeling as you do, you shall have a chance to examine their good points at close quarters."

Detesting the part he had to play, yet remembering Pan's declaration that it was the only possible way out, Teraf writhed with head on floor and tried to kiss the prodding foot.

"But my brother," he sobbed. "Surely Refo, your ally, would not wish . . ."

"Refo hates you. He thinks you smirched his betrothed and would delight to see you tied over an ant hill. But now let us question our beloved daughter." He sank back on the throne. "Pan Doh Ra, we absolve you in return for your having lured one of the most important Atlanteans to his doom as you promised you would do. Claims he's King of Hellas, doesn't he? What do you suggest that we do with such an honorable guest?"

"Oh, throw him to the 'dactyls for all I care." The girl

lifted one bare shoulder carelessly. "But not just yet. Let him suffer a little more first."

"Spoken like the true daughter of a pharaoh."

"I followed instructions pretty well, didn't I?" she preened. "It was easy. He's just another red fool like Zeus. But send him away now. His craven face nauseates me."

"Quite so." The Pharaoh grimaced with pleasure. Then, with another of his lightning changes of mood he added: "But just in case you take *us* for a fool, too, daughter, you will be confined to your room under close guard until the Hellene has been eaten."

Teraf was jerked to his feet and hustled out of the room. The sacred cat followed him to the door, yowling vindictively.

Chapter 12

No answer still. I thrust a torch through the remaining aperture and let it fall within. There came forth in return only a jingling of the bells. My heart grew sick . . . on account of the darkness of the catacombs. I hastened to make an end of my labor, I forced the last stone into its position; I plastered it up. Against the new masonry I re-erected the old rampart of bones. For the half of a century no mortal has disturbed them. In pace requiescat! *The Cask of Amontillado.* POE.

Out of the light of day, down through tier after tier of dungeons Teraf was pushed and prodded until a door clanged open and the guards thrust him headlong into his old cell.

"Beware the bars," warned one of the soldiers, "or you'll spoil the Pharaoh's fun."

As he rose to a sitting posture, his cellmates clustered 'round to hear of his experience. Their concerted movement must have roused the birds outside for the space behind the bars at once became crowded with solemn, horselike heads. After a moment of inspection the creatures, which had not yet been fed, hurled their bodies against the bars and thrust their long necks between them, snapping their teeth like pairs of scissors. Every space was filled, while Teraf and the others crouched against the farther wall, shaking as with ague.

They reminded him in some fantastic way of cows thrusting their heads through the bars of their mangers at milking time and this resemblance seemed at last to steady his nerves somewhat.

"Well, what did you learn?" Jason rasped when the commotion had died down somewhat.

Haltingly, the newcomer told of his interview.

"I thought so," grunted Nestor. "I also thought that girl was a spy who would betray us in the end. If you'd just listen to old Nestor."

"Shut up," snarled Teraf. "Shut up, all of you, unless you can suggest a way out of this mess."

"Well," sniggered the graybeard. "I think I do have something to contribute." He reached inside his filthy smock and pulled out a fluttering mass of feathers.

"What's that?" the others demanded in chorus.

"The last of the carrier pigeons. I saved it from the crate. We can still send a message to Atlan."

"And tell them to send a relief expedition," snorted Theseus. "Fat chance, with Bab El down."

"No, wait." Heracles screwed his face into a mask of concentration. "I think Hephaestus told me that in a few days he would have enough repairs made so he could get one ship into the air if he beamed all the power in one direction."

There were shouts of enthusiasm, but Teraf quelled them. "One ship," he snorted. "Do you think it can storm this place?"

"No, but . . ." Jason, thinking fast, strode up and down the narrow space in the cell which was safe from the 'dactyls. "No, but maybe we could ask the ship to hover until we managed to break out into the open some way. Then it could swoop down and pick us up. Surely, Teraf, one of the weapons Vanya gave you could help us."

"I have a package of acid," the Hellene admitted. "Perhaps I could cut the bars if those devils outside would give me a chance. But then what? Without our guns we would just be chicken feed, once we got outside."

"We'll be chicken feed in here pretty soon," said someone from the edge of the crowd. "I vote we give Nestor's idea a try." A shout of unanimous assent answered him.

As Nestor scribbled his S.O.S., Teraf carefully charted the area of safety in the cell. It was a space about ten feet wide and running the length of the room. Realizing that the horrors outside would be his playmates until he was cast to them, went mad, or managed to escape, he started pacing the cell, coming as near as he dared to the gnashing teeth.

He had become quite brave when there was a commotion in the line. One of the heads was jerked backward and another took its place. This 'dactyl was much larger and a lash of its whiplike neck sent the Hellene leaping for his life. He surveyed the newcomer thoughtfully. Pan Doh Ra had said there was only one such giant.

"Whoa, Sonny," he coaxed. "Wouldn't eat an old acquaintance, would you?"

The thing closed its jaws and regarded him sagely. Could it be, Teraf wondered, that such were the beasts which had given rise to the legend of the cockatrice—that flying reptile which could kill with a breath or a glance? Well, if looks or breaths could kill, he would already have been a long time dead, Teraf decided as he tried to stare down the long line of glaring eyes and was half-suffocated by their noxious exhalations. Only Sonny seemed in a receptive mood.

"I believe he recognizes me," muttered the prisoner and began a queer humming which he had learned from an Arabian jockey years ago. It was somewhat like Pan Doh Ra's keening and, if it worked with horses, why not with reptiles?

As he hummed, the line of hissing heads gradually subsided into silence, though the eyes still watched him hungrily. So far so good. Perhaps he could subdue the things as Pan Doh Ra had done. What did trainers say about looking wild beasts in the eye? But there were too many eyes for that.

Gingerly he approached Sonny, still keeping up his humming, and thrust a tentative hand toward the mouselike snout. The monster responded nobly by hurling himself against the bars and almost catching the hand in his yellow teeth.

"Too soon," chuckled a watching Argonaut. "But you're making progress. Keep it up and you'll have 'em all tamed—in a year or two."

Ignoring the remark, he started pacing again as he tried to puzzle out the last words of Pan Doh Ra. Was it a trick to fool her father—or had she achieved a neat double-cross? Well, he'd soon know if it was the latter. Guards would come presently to strip him of Vanya's packets. If not, there was still hope of escape.

The day waned without incident until Teraf and the others crouched in darkness, lighted only by glittering eyes and a dim murkiness toward the far end of the 'dactyl den. Evidently there was a barred gate or door from the den to the side of the cliff upon which the palace was built. He wished for a hand lantern so that he could explore the awful cavern with its beams.

Hours passed and no guards appeared. Then, just as his confidence in the princess was soaring, the lock of the cell grated and the corridor door swung open. But it was only a detail of bored soldiers bringing food and a candle. Their sergeant gave the Hellene to understand that the provisions were sent as a great favor, due to the high standing of the Argonauts. Most prisoners, they intimated, were allowed to starve or live on vermin in the dark.

After that the little company lost count of the hours. They slept fitfully, waking in a cold sweat many times after dreaming that they had rolled from the far wall within reach of the waiting beaks. The light was there again when they awoke as the door opened to admit more food and a pitifully scant supply of water.

The second day, when the monsters had somewhat lost interest and hung themselves head downward from their perches, Teraf decided the time had come for action. With much twisting and cursing he managed to tear the package of acid from his chest. Working carefully by the light of the flaring candle he mixed some of the powdered contents with water. He found a needle that had been packed with the acid and, timing himself so as not to be interrupted by the guards, started work on the bars.

At first he aroused the interest of the reptiles, which dived at him whenever he approached the wall. But gradually they went back to sleep and he worked undisturbed, cutting the metal bars almost through near the floor. His comrades offered to relieve him after long hours of lying on his belly had made the work almost unendurable, but whenever a new face approached the lattice the 'dactyls went wild and the volunteer had to retire.

After a day of toil, made more difficult by the raging thirst from which he and the others now suffered, the task was finished. Five bars were weakened so that a quick lunge near the floor would break them. Teraf was so pleased while inspecting his success that a black shape crept upon him and managed to slash his shoulder before he could roll to safety. The wound was slight, however. After cauterizing it with a weak solution of acid, he crouched down beside the others to wait.

To wait for what? Even if Pan Doh Ra were loyal to Atlan, she was locked in her room.

"And if the pigeon got through," growled Theseus, "who knows whether a ship could be sent, or how long it will wait for a signal from us."

Time passed. Interminable hours. Days. In their half-stupor they even imagined that weeks had gone by. Conversation lagged. The dice games petered out. The odor from the den stifled them. The coarse food and inadequate water nauseated and infuriated them. The ambassador died, and they actually sighed with relief when his ravings were heard no more. Some of the prisoners began holding long, obscene conversations with the monsters which still inspected them wistfully just before feeding time.

Those feeding periods brought their own particular horror. At the clang of a gong, the distant door at the outer side of the den would swing open and several shrieking unfortunates would be thrust through it. With a great flapping of wings and gnashing of teeth, the 'dactyls would drop from their perches and race for the living food. Sometimes victims would escape for a time by dashing round and round the den. Once a poor wretch clung to the bars of the cell, screaming, until he was slashed to fragments. After that, Teraf gave orders for the Argonauts to bury their heads in their filthy blankets during this ordeal.

Time dragged on—with no message. But one night, when the Hellene was debating whether he should not poison his companions with the remains of the acid, and put them out of their misery, the corridor door creaked and opened, inch by inch.

"Pan Doh Ra?" whispered Teraf.

There was no answer, except the sound of stealthy footsteps.

"Who goes there?" he rasped, thinking that perhaps Plu Toh Ra had decided to get rid of them at once and was opening the gate into the den.

"It is us, Medea," came the answer then. "For Isis' sake, be silent."

A tall, black-draped figure slipped through the door. Behind it came a much smaller shadow, also draped in black. The door swung shut, leaving them standing in the light of the guttering candle.

Teraf leaned over and shook Jason awake. Whatever happened from now on, he surmised, would be up to the handsome captain.

Jason responded nobly. "Medea—darling," he breathed. "You have come to save us."

"Perhaps," she answered, and Teraf thought he caught a faint flicker of amusement in her tone. The woman was no one's fool.

"You do love me then?" Jason implored. "I was sure I saw it in your eyes."

This was going pretty fast, but Teraf dared say nothing.

"Maybe," she replied. "As a princess I have never had an

opportunity to know real love until now. . . . Are the rest asleep?"

"All but Teraf, I think."

"Very well, then. Listen." She crouched down beside us. "Perhaps we love you, Jason. We do not know. But you affect us strangely . . . here." She touched her heart. "Or perhaps it is because we know much of ancient magic and can read in the stars that Atlantis is strong—strong. Or—still another perhaps—we do not desire longer to be subject to the whims of our brother, who has transferred all of his affections to his cub in recent days." Her voice rang like bells on a frosty night. "Tell me, Jason, if you escaped and got back to Atlan on the ship which circles high above Sais, would you be rewarded?"

"I had had no thought of that."

"Jason will be rewarded," Teraf interrupted. "Iberia has had no king since the death of Cadmus."

"And might we be Queen of Iberia if Jason were king?"

"I'll vouch for that, especially if he brings back his comrades and—and the orichalcum which Plu Toh Ra stole."

"We cannot bring you the burning metal." She started to rise, and said, "But we can tell you much about the disposition of Egypt's armed forces."

"So be it." The Hellene found himself adopting this high faluting way of talking. "If it suits Jason, I think you may become an Iberian queen."

"It will suit Jason," she purred as she lowered crossed arms to disclose the guns of the Argonauts, which she had been carrying in her mantle.

"And who is that with you?" Teraf asked.

"It is our younger brother, Absyrtus, whom we have brought along as a hostage." She threw back a fold of cloth to disclose the face of a sleepy boy about twelve years old.

Teraf shook the rest of the company awake and had a hard time keeping them from having hysterics when he distributed the weapons. Next he ordered them to make improvised gas masks by tearing their blankets into strips and dipping the cloth in the last of their water. And finally he ordered Jason, Heracles, Theseus and two lesser strong men to go to work on the bars. Heracles was through in a jiffy and back to help the others who were having difficulty bending the massive metal strips.

They had thought the pterodactyls were asleep, but no! Squealing and snapping, they began dropping from their perches for an attack.

"But how can we signal the ship?" puzzled the big engineer. "We have no flares."

"Fire thunderbolts three times at the zenith," Teraf barked. "That should bring them."

For a long moment—just long enough for the 'dactyls to get under way—the guns traced fifty lines of scarlet into the night sky. Then they were forced to concentrate on targets nearer at hand.

Flesh shriveled and stank as the flying horde swept down. But, being reptiles with very low order nervous systems, they did not seem to know when they had been killed. Even with wings, legs, and parts of their bodies burned away, they swept on to overwhelm the humans. It was only a matter of seconds before naught would be left of the Argonauts.

They did not despair, however, for the Atlantean ship had received their signal, had spotted them and was dropping swiftly toward the center of the courtyard, spraying the scene with the brilliance of its searchlights. Yet it would be nip and tuck. The 'dactyls were closing in fast and it seemed impossible that fifty-three persons could squeeze through the ship's hatch before many had been torn to shreds.

Teraf heard Medea, running beside him, draw in her breath with a sharp hiss. "Here then," she snarled. "We always hated the brat anyway."

Before he could make a move to stop her, she seized the boy Absyrtus in her strong, round arms, swung him over her head and hurled him straight into the midst of the onrushing monsters.

That stopped them, but only for a shriek-filled moment which gave the ship an opportunity to land. Then, looking like rearing winged horses or blacksheeted specters, the beasts once more loomed above their cursing victims as the latter finally broke in panic and sprinted for the hatch.

At that, Teraf played his last card. Ripping off the third packet without noticing the skin which came with it, he shouted a warning against gas, then hurled the contents as far as possible.

Though they were almost immune to blasting, the 'dacytls were in difficulty as soon as the powder disintegrated into a cloud of white, phosphorescent vapor. They fluttered and flopped, for all the world like chickens with their heads cut off. Their wings, beating in the agony of suffocation, quickly spread the gas to all parts of the chamber. A few continued to strike at the enemy and even at each other, but their movements had become wildly uncoordinated.

But now a new danger threatened. Aroused by the commotion, the palace guard came pouring into the courtyard. They were well-armed with stolen Atlantean weapons and looked like animated mummies in the gas masks they had delayed to improvise. The guards charged in wedge formation, their guns slashing viciously at the few Argonauts still outside the ship.

"Take her up," shouted Teraf as he pushed the laggards inside. He reached for the hand rail to hoist himself aboard. . . .

The Hellene recovered consciousness with the conviction that he had died and been thrown into a sewer. He could see nothing, and all about him was a stench which passed all understanding. He tried to move but was confined by some wet rubbery substance. His head ached as though it had been beaten with a hammer.

"How many of them did we get?" The Egyptian words came muffled and faint.

"Twelve of the bustards. But they killed every 'dactyl in the yard. Take a good long look at the sun, Turo. The Pharaoh will make certain that you never see it rise again."

"But I thought I tagged their leader, just as the ship rose," came the answer in the unhappiest of voices. "If I could just find his body, the Pharaoh might relent enough to just cut off my hand or something. Where in Tophet did that Hellene get to?"

"Maybe the 'dactyls tore him to pieces in their death struggles after he fell. I'll call slaves to clear the den."

"I'll go with you. This stink turns my stomach."

The voices receded and Teraf, aware now of his true condition, fought blindly to crawl from under the reptilian corpse which was lying across his body. Finally he pushed aside a crumpled wing and peered about him. The guards were just re-entering their quarters and, for a moment, the courtyard was given over to its dead.

He started to rise, then sank back with a groan. The bolt which had creased his temple still had him groggy. And what was the use of further struggle? His fate was sealed when the slaves came and discovered him.

Then, when hope seemed dead, a monster to the right of him stirred and coughed ever so slightly. A moment later it tried to heave itself from among its suffocated fellows and, by the light of torches which the guards had posted on the walls, he recognized it by its giant size as Sonny, Pan Doh Ra's pet.

A desperate plan forming in his mind, Teraf wriggled free and crawled toward the reviving brute. Recalling that the princess once had told him that pterodactyls could not dislodge or strike at a rider on their backs, he rose, tottered forward and fell between the wildly flopping wings. As he had suspected, those wings were hobbled. He tore at the thongs until his fingers bled, got them untied at last and began beating at Sonny's sagging head and neck, drumming on its ribs with his heels.

"Sonny! Sonny Boy," he gabbled. "Get me out of here, old timer."

He fought his numbed brain in an effort to remember the tone Pan Doh Ra had used in humming to her pets. Was it C or F? He tried F.

The animal beneath him struggled with more vigor. Its neck lifted. Its wings flapped wildly, stirring up a storm of dust.

A shout from the guardhouse told him that his efforts had been noticed. Seizing a stone, he hammered Sonny over the head with it.

The brute screamed in pain. Its wings roared. Just as one of the approaching guards lashed out at it with his sword the last of the pterodactyls took to the air in crazy, lopsided flight, with the half-conscious King of Hellas clinging to its back.

Chapter 13

For there was a time, Solon, before the great deluge of all, when the city which now is Athens, was first in war and in every way the best governed of all cities, and is said to have performed the noblest deeds and to have had the fairest constitution of any of which tradition tells under the face of heaven. PLATO's *Timaeus.*

For hours Sonny flapped dazedly northwestward while Teraf lay between his wings, almost unconscious. Then the deadening effect of the poison wore off and the Hellene felt almost himself again except for a splitting headache.

At the same time his steed became restless. Again and again it cast a baleful eye back at him as if puzzling how a stranger had got on its back. Then it began to snap and scratch at him; but teeth and claws could not quite reach their objective. So it started diving and rolling in an effort to dislodge him, but this proved equally futile.

At last Sonny started a rapid glide. Teraf tried coaxing, belaboring and crooning, but the beast kept sliding down the air like a shadow in the setting sun.

They were over a great forest now. According to the prince's hazy reckoning, he was far beyond the confines of Egypt and in the kingdom of Crete or even Hellas. But there was nothing hazy about the fact that Sonny was seeking a clearing in which to land and rid himself of his rider. He swept low over the trees; but as he passed not ten feet above the top of a huge pine, Teraf slipped from his perch, trusting to fate to afford him a grip on some branch.

He succeeded and some minutes later was crouched at the bottom of the pine, bruised and breathless, but rid of flying reptiles. The 'dactyl's thirty foot wings had made it impossible for him to invade the underbrush in search of his prey.

The Hellene had escaped one peril, however, only to fall into another. In the forest it was already quite dark and the night life had begun to awake. Far away he heard the laughter of a giant jackal. Near at hand sounded the pad, pad, of some beast looking for supper. Teraf thanked heaven that he had dropped out of the sky and therefore had no trail of scent to betray him.

But a night spent in the open did not intrigue him; he was ready to drop from fatigue and the aftereffects of the gas. And, if he stayed where he was, he could not hope to escape for long the attentions of jackals, five-foot-tall timber wolves and worse yet, saber-tooth tigers—those terrors of hunters from one end of Atlantis to the other.

Fearfully he left what little protection the tree afforded and walked slowly forward, hoping to see some sign of a clearing. He was not successful in this, but, instead, caught sight of a tiny gleam of yellow light in the distance. It blinked a friendly welcome as he stumbled toward it.

Around him, the forest had come alive with the screams and snarls of animals either pursued or pursuing. Once he imagined he heard some beast snuffling at his heels and had to fight down an insane desire to dash wildly and noisily toward the light. But he held himself in check until he reached the door of a rough cabin, through the chinks of which a lamp was twinkling.

He knocked. A wrinkled face, topped by a mass of touseled white hair, surveyed him for a long moment through a barred wicket. Then a bar was lifted.

"Welcome to the hut of Hardish, the charcoal burner," cackled the old man as Teraf entered blinking. " 'Tis a long, long way you must have come this day. And wearing the garb of an Atlantean, too. It's been months since I had such a pleasure. Seat yourself, sir. You must be hungry. I have little enough, but you are welcome."

Hardish brought dried meat, nuts, berries and coarse bread. These he set before his exhausted guest, as Teraf huddled on a rude bench beside the roaring fire.

Teraf ate ravenously, stopping from time to time to answer as best he could the questions of the charcoal burner. He remained reticent about most of his own adventures, but was forced to admit that he had fallen from the back of a tamed pterodactyl while en route from Sais . . . here he stumbled slightly . . . to Atlan.

"He! He! And 'tis far off your course you are," snickered the hermit. "I'm told there's war between Egypt and Atlan, too. Well! Well! It's no soot off my fingers if they kill each other." And, as Teraf's head drooped, he added: "I'll fix your bed. You look half dead."

Hobbling about with remarkable agility for his age, Hardish spread a pallet of straw and furs on the floor. Teraf's head hardly had touched the pillow before he was asleep.

He dreamed that once more he was lying paralyzed in the Cave of the Oracle, and awoke to find his dream come true; try as he would, he could not move hand nor foot. Had the after-effects of the gas paralyzed his nerve centers? Sheer horror gripped him and turned his bones to water.

He squirmed desperately. Managing to lift his head, he discovered that he was not paralyzed but instead was strapped tightly to a board. Rolling his eyes, he made out the hermit seated on a nearby bench, hands between knees and rocking with silent mirth.

"He! He!" the old man chortled. "Thought I was a half-wit, didn't ye? Thought I wouldn't know you for a damned Atlantean spy sent to find out what he could about our great King Refo and his plans? Heigh ho! I shall turn a pretty penny by taking you to Athens."

Hardish left off his rocking and jerked aside a leathern curtain. Behind it was revealed a tiny vision screen.

"Oh, I've been listening," he jeered. "I know all about the war. Zeus and his cursed foreigners have their backs to the wall. They would bring in all that electricity and spoil a poor old charcoal burner's means of making a living, would they? He! He! But I'm busier than ever these last few weeks."

Teraf kept silent under this tirade, knowing that nothing could move the old man. Hardish also became silent at last. Rising, he dragged his prisoner out of the cabin and, with much pulling and puffing, loaded him like a sack of grain or charcoal into a waiting ox cart.

For two endless days the wooden-wheeled vehicle bumped slowly over the rough byways of Hellas. Fearful that his precious prisoner might be taken from him by the military, Hardish drove to Athens by a roundabout way which almost shook Teraf's bones through his skin.

But the hermit was careful of his victim's health. At night he stopped, loosened the bonds somewhat, cooked food and mocked the Hellene until he dropped off to sleep. In vain Teraf tried pleadings, bribery and threats. The old man almost went into hysterics when he finally revealed that he was Refo's brother.

"He! He! So I have caught a king," he sniggered. "Well, you are in good company. I am your long-lost grandfather."

After an infinity of such agony the prisoner perceived through the cracks in the side of the cart that they were entering the capital. Quite different from arriving at the head of a conquering army, he groaned. Oh, well—anything was better than this eternal jolting.

Hardish drove up to the gates of the palace before being accosted. There he turned his sooty captive over to the guard and hobbled excitedly after them, demanding payment for his trouble, as they carried Teraf inside.

No one recognized the rightful king, of course, and he was placed in a cell to await Refo's disposal. Released from his bonds, he could not stand at first, while returning circulation made him sweat with pain. At last, however, he managed to eat and drink and fell into a troubled slumber. He was awakened when a kilted soldier shook him.

"The king would have speech with you. Arise!" commanded the guard.

Wondering what the next act of the drama would be, Teraf gathered his rags about him, stumbled to his feet and was ushered from the cell through a long, cool corridor and into the throne room.

The serene beauty of the place enthralled him as it had in his childhood. It did not imitate the grandeur of Olympus, but achieved its effect by long sweeping lines, simple Ionic columns and marbles so beautiful that they seemed almost to breathe.

On a dais near an arch overlooking the mountains sat the king. He was dressed, not in court vestments, but in a simple white tunic. His chin rested on one hand as he stared into the distance, apparently oblivious of the prisoner. At last, however, he turned tired eyes toward Teraf. For a moment he stared at the dirty specter who stood before him, then leaped to his feet.

"Hail, your majesty." Teraf achieved a grin. "Receive our kingly blessing."

"What do you mean by bringing a prince of Hellas to me in this condition?" Refo stormed at the guards. "Go! Prepare baths. Bring food and clothing. Brother, rest yourself. We will talk later."

"We will talk now, if you please." The grin was gone.

Impatiently the king waved away his attendants. When they were alone he drew his brother to a seat beside him on the throne. He either ignored or had forgotten the bitterness of their last meeting.

"The only chance I may ever have of sitting here," chuckled Teraf. "Well, brother. Speak up."

"I'm sorry for what has happened, but it cannot be undone," the king began without preamble. "Sometimes I think I was a fool and that my people would be better off as well-fed slaves of the Martians than as starving freemen.

"But I have put my hand to the plough. There will be a period of struggle and readjustment after we win, but the Pharaoh and I have pledged ourselves to give independence to all minority peoples."

"Fair words," grunted Teraf. "But in the meantime your subjects are hungry."

"Yes. I know." Refo shifted uneasily. "With the destruction of Bab El all our factories have stopped. I am besieged by starving people on the streets." He passed a hand over his face as if to brush away an evil dream.

"It's not too late to turn back," Teraf insisted. "Zeus will forgive you, even now. As for Plu Toh Ra, he's a lying son of a scarab and not to be trusted." He then outlined his recent experiences in Sais.

"But you disgraced his daughter!" Refo's face began to darken with the old, unreasoning anger.

"It's a lie . . . a lie deliberately told to make us hate each other. Ask the daughter, not the father. She's everything he's not."

"I don't believe you." But Refo's anger had died away. "Anyway, I have given my word to Plu Toh Ra."

All of Teraf's hopes were blasted by those last words. He well knew the old code of honor which had been handed down by the kings of Hellas since before the dawn of history. "Then what becomes of me?" he muttered as he bowed his head in defeat.

"I am not an Egyptian. You'll be escorted to Atlan—on one condition."

"And that is?"

"That you give your word never to lead an army against your native land while I live."

It was Teraf's turn to ponder. Would he be of more use in Atlan under the crippling oath, or free to do as he pleased—in an Athenean prison?

"I promise," he said at last, placing his hand on the back of the great throne as was the ancient custom. "And may whatever gods there be have mercy on your soul."

"I ask for no mercy," sighed the king. "If I have done wrong, I will pay the penalty.

"And now I must leave you," he continued, rising and changing in the instant from a sorely puzzled man into the vibrant and kingly personality who radiated self-confidence, and whom the people loved.

"Bathe, eat, sleep and put on new clothing. Tomorrow you shall go to Atlan. If we never meet again . . . farewell."

For a moment he gripped his brother's shoulders with both hands, then hurried out of the hall without a backward glance.

Chapter 14

And the woman said, The serpent beguiled me. *Genesis.*

Four days later Teraf stood before Zeus and the Council, giving a report of his adventures. Cheers greeted his description of the passing of the flying reptiles. A few chuckles were heard when he related how he had been captured by a charcoal burner. Zeus and Athena nodded sympathetically when he told of Refo's unhappiness.

"We may save the boy yet," said the Pitar.

"I overheard whispers among members of my escort," said the Hellene, "that when Refo left me, he departed in all haste for Sais."

"Now what devil's work are they up to?" growled Hephaestus, and added: "A thorough check at Bab El discloses five more ounces of orichalcum missing. If it has been smuggled through our lines . . ."

"A cat couldn't get out of the city," snapped Ares.

"Teraf, you haven't heard of this," interrupted the Pitar. "A young engineer—Marco by name—disappeared from Bab El three days ago, simultaneously with the orichalcum Hephaestus speaks of."

"A most suicidal thing to do," fumed the crippled engineer. "Since the first theft, we have stripped and searched each employee as he left the station. If Marco stole the stuff, he must have held it in his mouth in a very thin container. Let's say he kept it there ten minutes—it would have caused a terrible, slow-developing burn which must have killed him in two days. You know how devilish a burn from radioactive material can be. Too bad. Marco was a nice boy."

"Then you're searching for a dead man?" queried Teraf.

"Ares and Hermes are cooperating on that," Zeus nodded. "Have either of you anything to report?"

The warlord shook his head gloomily.

"I have a clue, sir," Hermes stammered, "but, ah, I'd rather not discuss it now. If I can just prowl about the palace and grounds for a few days I think I can at least produce what's left of Marco."

As Teraf left the chamber, the chronicler dropped in beside him and slipped an arm through his. "Say, king, may I have an audience?"

The Hellene nodded and, without another word, they traversed the long corridor and entered Teraf's suite. There the chronicler poured himself a stiff drink and collapsed into his customary contortion on the most comfortable chair.

"I need your help in trailing Aphrodite," he began at last. "I have a hunch she had a hand in those thefts. Been watching her, ever since the last one. I haven't got anything on her yet, but right now is the first time she's been out of my sight this week."

"That's a pretty serious charge against poor old Zeus' pet daughter."

"Well, look at it this way. She disappeared after the first batch of orichalcum vanished. Then, I've learned that she had been vamping Marco."

"But what on earth could be her motive?"

"Here's the dope as well as I can get it. I picked it up from all sorts of places. The morgue over at the *Planet*—newspaper gossip. . . . You know. . . .

"Two years ago Aphrodite paid a visit to Sais . . . stayed there several months. At the time it was rumored that Plu Toh Ra might take her as his queen. Nothing came of it, so far as anybody knew. But she returned to Atlan with the idea that Martians were too wrapped up in business and colonization to pay any attention to the more esthetic things of life.

"Later she decided she wanted to be a 'business woman' too—wanted to amount to something like Athena. A complete change of heart, you see. She then went up to Bab El and studied for a time under Hephaestus, who adores her, the sentimental old fool. Flubbed her electronics in grand style, of course, and wound up by having violent flirtations with members of the staff. . . ."

Automatically Hermes' hand went out, only to discover that the decanter was empty.

"I'll ring for another," said his intrigued host.

"Never mind. Never mind. I have a hunch. Let's try out this freedom of the palace which the Old Boy has granted me. Heracles was telling me there's a bottle or two of Iberian nectar in the cellars that have been gathering cobwebs since Poseidon's time. What say we broach them?" Of a sudden the reporter was vibrating with energy.

A gnome-like cellarman let them pass into the wine vaults without question, then trailed after them like a misshapen ghost.

"Why don't you ask him where it is?" queried Teraf, staring helplessly at the array of bottles, barrels and kegs which surrounded them.

"Nuh uh! More fun to look!"

As they turned into an ill-lighted, cobwebby corridor the gnome skipped into the lead and blocked their way with long, outstretched arms. "Can't go there, my masters," he bawled.

"And why not, you long-eared bat?" Hermes gripped him by the shoulder.

"Orders from the Pitar, masters. I have them here."

He thrust a hand under his leather jerkin. It came forth holding a curved blade with which he slashed viciously at his captor.

Hermes slumped to the floor. Before there was time for the blow to be repeated Teraf brought a bottle down on the cellarman's head. The gnome collapsed across the body of his victim, bathed in the foam of vintage champagne.

"Don't wait," gasped the chronicler as Teraf bent over him. "You'll find Aphrodite down that corridor, I think. She wasn't at the council meeting, remember. . . . Great Land of Nod, king, stop pawing me! The future of Atlan may depend . . ." He fainted.

Snatching the cellarman's lantern, Teraf raced down the narrow passageway. Far in front he thought he caught a flash of white. He redoubled his pace.

The white patch doubled a corner. He skidded after it.

"Don't come a step nearer," panted a frightened voice. "I —I have you covered."

Teraf hurled himself headfirst at the shadowy figure ahead. They went down in a tangle, the gun sparkling harmlessly.

"Let me go, you filthy Alfha!" The woman he had pinioned twisted and bit like a panther.

Seizing both her wrists with one hand, Teraf at last retrieved the lantern with the other and flashed its light on her face.

It was Aphrodite, of course, but a changed Aphrodite. Her face was almost as white as his own, now. Her mouth was drawn into a square through which tiny teeth gleamed. Her eyes showed mere greenish slits. "Zeus shall hear of this," she hissed.

"So he shall." Teraf released her and picked up the gun. "Now march in front of me quietly or you will return to the sea foam from which the silly poets say you came."

Her mood changed. Bowing her head she begged and pleaded as she stumbled along before him.

"Got her?" queried a weak voice as they approached the end of the corridor.

"You bet." Teraf breathed a sigh of relief to find the reporter conscious again. "Can you hold out till I come back?"

"Sure. I'm bleeding a bit, but I'm hard to kill. Take her to Zeus yourself. She'll bribe or seduce the guards. Hurry . . . back."

The Hellene dashed for the cellar entrance, now dragging his sobbing captive behind him. Up the stairs he stumbled, and burst into the audience chamber to find the Pitar surrounded by a sea of war maps. Despite Aphrodite's hysterical screams he told his story.

Zeus' face mottled. He rang for the guard, then caught his daughter in his arms as she fainted gracefully.

"Get Hermes to a doctor," he snapped. "If the cellarman is alive, lock him up. Then take a squad and search that corridor. I'll take care of this."

Collecting men-at-arms as he ran, Teraf rushed back into the cellar. The gnome still lay across the body of the chronicler; he was dead. Hermes was unconscious again but his wound, though deep, had not penetrated a vital organ. Teraf had him carried above post-haste.

With five men at his back, the Hellene then went down the

fatal corridor until he reached a dead end. There the lanterns revealed that the flooring had been torn up and clumsily replaced. Under the dirt was Marco.

Far back, behind a row of tall bottles, they at last discovered a heavy lead container in which all or part of the missing orichalcum was now enclosed.

Dispatching this to the Pitar, Teraf hurried to the palace hospital. Hermes welcomed him with his usual quizzical grin.

"I'm still in one piece, king," he whispered. "Vanya will have me up in about a week or I'll skin him. Check up and see if the cellarman wasn't a relative of Marco's. Seems to me I remember something about a deformed brother. . . . That's why we went down there in such a hurry. I got to figuring that Aphrodite would make a break for the cellar as soon as she thought I wasn't shadowing her." He yawned and went to sleep forthwith.

In the audience chamber the council had been hurriedly reassembled. Hephaestus, his wrinkled face twisted by grief and disbelief, sat on the edge of a chair, staring alternately at his gnarled, scarred hands and at his former protege. Heracles lounged uncomfortably in his corner. Athena was helping a nurse to restore consciousness to the captive.

As Teraf entered, Aphrodite opened her wonderful eyes.

"I didn't do it, father," she wailed like a little girl. "I was just looking for a bottle of wine. Teraf frightened me." She beat her round breasts with clenched fists.

"Let me see those hands," commanded the Pitar.

"I—I burned them. Scalded them while washing my hair. They're not pretty." She hid them behind her back.

"You never washed your own hair in your life." Zeus jerked the offending hands into the light. The palms were blistered and seared.

"Typical orichalcum burn," Hephaestus gulped. "She probably got it putting the material in the big container."

"Aphrodite, look at me!" The Pitar took the broken woman by the shoulders. "Enough of your lies. I know there is one thing that you fear above all others. That is death! Now tell us why you did this foul thing."

As she comprehended his meaning, the once-proud darling of the court whimpered and prepared to faint again. Her father shook her roughly. At this she recovered herself. Her eyes became stony, her mouth tense. "Will I be pardoned if I tell everything?" she bargained.

"You'll not die."

For a long moment she stared down at her ruby-studded sandals, then threw back her head defiantly. "Yes, I had Marco steal the orichalcum for me," she cried. "He loved me. He hid it in his mouth. He died for me. He was a man, not a machine."

"He's neither now," breathed Zeus. "Proceed. Why did Plu Toh Ra want the stuff?"

"Plu Toh Ra?" She hesitated. Her glance wavered.

"To blow up Atlan," she replied at last.

"Heracles," snapped the Pitar, "wring my daughter's pretty neck for me."

The giant lunged forward, apparently unmoved by the strange command, his hairy hands extended like hams.

Aphrodite screamed. Her eyes started from her head.

"Not that! Not that!" she gabbled. "I'll tell everything. Plu Toh Ra plans to capture the dam at the Pillars of Heracles and blow it up if you refuse to surrender. The orichalcum—except the little used to bomb Atlan—has been made into a bomb which will be held as a sword over you."

"And you connived in this?"

"Oh, God, yes. Plu Toh Ra loves me as I always wanted to be loved. He, too, is a man. You others are mere slaves and drudges. He will marry me . . . make me his queen . . . have me worshipped as a goddess in Sais. He . . ."

"Shut up, strumpet!" Zeus whirled on the council. "There's not a moment to lose," he thundered. "Even now the Pharaoh may be on his way. That visit from Refo which Teraf has told us of is probably the prelude to an attack. If the dam is taken we're helpless. If it is broken, the waters of the Atlantic will sweep over all of Atlan, drowning it hundreds of feet deep. None will escape."

There was a bull roar of fury from the corner into which Heracles had retreated. "It's my dam." The giant's eyes were wild. "I built it. And, by the fifteen little demons, I'll save it."

Zeus shook his head. "Iberia is almost a wilderness," he said soothingly. "Those who go will have to travel much of the way on horseback. Your weight would kill any horse in half a day's ride. And then, I'd rather keep you here. It's war to the death now and I'll need every engineer in Atlan.

"Teraf, you've had experience traveling through rough country. You start at once. A regiment of cavalry will follow, but you must get to the dam first and warn the guard. Plu Toh Ra is jamming our radio station with his own at Sais so we can't get through that way.

"Take the fastest motor car at the palace. Quite a number

of the internal combustion kind have been taken out of museums and reconditioned. No airplanes have been made ready for service yet or we wouldn't be in this mess." He glared at Apollo, who spread his slim hands helplessly.

"The roads are good about half the way from here to the dam. After that you'll have to trust to luck and ingenuity. Apollo, give him gold for the purchase of horses.

"Probably the Egyptians have one or two days' start, but they have farther to go and must take a roundabout course. They may have a few internal combustion cars. Their pterodactyls are dead, you say, and their planes can't operate without power from Bab El.

"Now go, with our blessing. There'll be others following you, so don't hesitate to take chances. Don't think of your own life. Think of Atlan. Let us hope this is not farewell."

He gripped Teraf by the hand and there were tears in his tired eyes.

Chapter 15

In Egypt we have the oldest of the Old World children of Atlantis; in her magnificence we have a testimony to the development attained by the parent country; by that country whose kings were the gods of succeeding nations, and whose kingdom extended to the uttermost ends of the earth. IGNATIUS DONNELLY'S *Atlantis.*

In Sais, the arrival of Refo had brought on a climax the day before Aphrodite's treason had been revealed in Atlan.

Dusty and tired, the King of Hellas strode into the Pharaoh's presence unannounced. He found the Egyptian lecturing his daughter on her unseemly conduct. (The visit of the Princess Medea to Teraf in the dungeons had been hushed up by the simple method of poisoning all the soldiers and priests who had been witness to it.)

Declaring that he would give her one more chance to act as a member of the royal household should, Plu Toh Ra had by this time placed his daughter on probation—that is, had given her the freedom of the palace. But this kindness was more than compensated for by the daily lectures which he made her endure.

When the black-haired northerner burst into the shadowed throne room, Pan Doh Ra rose. Without a glance or word she marched into her apartment and slammed the door.

"Pardon my daughter," said the ruler with a thin smile. "Her manners, and those of other members of my house, are not of the best—a fault which we shall now remedy." He rose to follow the girl.

"Stop," barked Refo. "This is no time to discipline wayward daughters. Is the bomb finished?"

His deep voice penetrated faintly through the massive door of the princess' quarters. Abandoning her intention to put as much space as possible between herself and her former betrothed, Pan Doh Ra placed one pink ear to the jamb.

"Not so loud," cautioned the Egyptian. "Walls have ears, even in Sais. Ha! A clever phrase!" He glanced about for a scribe, then, since none was present, scratched the deathless words on a piece of papyrus.

"Yes," he said as he concluded. "The bomb is completed. A Martian engineer we kidnaped was induced to bring his labors to a close yesterday. . . . He may live for some time, they say. . . . His bomb is a work of art. We used all the orichalcum at hand and will have to depend on that silly fool, Aphrodite, to provide us with more—if more should be needed."

"We must depart at once for the dam, then," Refo interrupted. "My spies at Atlan say Bab El will be repaired within the fortnight. That will place so much power in Hephaestus' hands that our cause will become hopeless.

"If we attempt to reach the dam after the tower is restored, the Pitar will know of it by radio at once, for your jamming will then be futile. Unless we go with an army then, we would be arrested in one of the African colonies. If we strike now we have our only chance at surprise and success."

Outside the throne room door, Pan Doh Ra trembled at his words and her hands clenched fiercely. She knew well enough what capture of the dam would mean to Atlan.

"Perhaps you have heard"—the Pharaoh was speaking now—"that that renegade brother of yours succeeded in poisoning all of our pterodactyls except one on which he escaped from the dungeon. Our perfidious sister escaped with other Martians and Titans in an airship, which achieved the impossible by reaching Sais. We do not think that ship succeeded in making the return journey to Atlan. Search parties are out."

"Nephele, too?" Refo muttered.

The Pharaoh chose not to hear that remark.

"We'll have to use a motor car to reach the dam, and depend on horses if it breaks down."

"Teraf told me of his coup when he reached Athens," Refo interrupted with a bitter smile.

"Then he's dead!" The Egyptian pushed his ubiquitous cat aside and leaped to his feet with blazing eyes.

"Dead? Oh, I didn't have him killed, if that's what you mean. I haven't yet descended to fratricide."

"You're a sentimental fool. Well, at least he's safely imprisoned."

"No, I sent him to Atlan after he promised never to lead an attack on Hellas."

The Pharaoh's jaw fell. He collapsed upon his throne. On the other side of the chamber door, Pan Doh Ra felt an icy hand relax its grip on her heart.

"You half-wit," the monarch raged. "You triple-distilled idiot. The Martians should decorate you for that deed!" He stared at his ally through slitted eyes and added: "I wonder if you are not secretly in league with Atlan."

During this harangue the cat had been creeping toward the Hellene on its golden belly. Now, fur bristling and tail switching madly, it snarled and spat at Refo with a fury equal to that of its master.

By this time the Egyptian had worked himself into a frenzy. His eyes rolled. A fleck of spittle appeared on his lips. "When an empire is at stake you let sentiment override common sense," he screamed. "Coward! Traitor! Sw—"

At the beginning of this tirade, Refo had stood as one turned to marble; as it proceeded the blood drained from his face. Now, as the Pharaoh's lips opened to utter the final insult, he leaped forward, kicked the clawing feline out of his way and gripped his fellow conspirator by the shoulders.

"By Gaea and Chronus," he gritted. "Another word and I'll kill you though I be slashed to mincemeat by your guards afterward."

Fascinated by the drama unfolding in the royal chamber, the princess had opened her door slightly and placed an eye to the crack. As Refo spoke, she saw her father's rage drain slowly from him, like wine from a cracked vase. Finally he laughed shakily, though his eyes retained their wild glint.

"Forgive us, friend," he muttered. "We are often carried away of late by these fits of passion. It is the strain of waiting. They mean nothing. Forget what we have said. Come." He straightened his great shoulders. "We start for the Pillars of Heracles at once."

As he spoke his roving eyes lit on the door from behind which his daughter was peeping. With the spring of a forest animal he gained the portal and threw it open, knocking the girl to the floor.

"Ignoble! Ignoble!" he raged again. "Oh, Isis and Osiris, what have we done that our own daughter should spy on us." He beat the heavy gold collar around his neck with jeweled hands.

"Up, Alfha brat!" He stirred the cowering girl with the toe of his sandal. "You are no longer our daughter. We have no time to deal with you now. When we return we shall have the pleasure of cropping those pretty ears. Until then . . ."

He returned to the throne, picked up the cat, which was still whimpering with terror from Refo's kick, placed it gently on the floor inside his daughter's room, then shut and bolted the door.

"Horus will see that she gets into no more mischief." He grinned wryly. Then to Refo, "You are lucky that we discovered her nature in time. Now follow us."

For hours, Pan Doh Ra lay upon a divan to which she had dragged herself after the door was locked, staring dry-eyed out of the barred window. At last she got up and, closely followed by the limping Horus, once more made the dreary round of the apartment which had served as her prison since, as a tiny girl, she had thrown mud at a stately high priest of Osiris, thereby forcing him to spend a ten day period in purification.

The memory of that delicious incident served to revive her spirits somewhat. Even as a child she had hated those shaven-pated men who, by means of their prophecies, influenced her father's every mood and action. As a grubby tomboy of ten she had been particularly affronted because they trod solemnly about in robes so immaculate that it was considered a defilement if so much as a fly lighted upon them.

Automatically she tried the bars of various slitted windows, but they held fast as she knew they would. So she resigned herself to another period of semistarvation unless her old nurse dared to smuggle her something more substantial than bread and water.

The cat also seemed satisfied with the results of the inspection and retreated purring into a corner. There it sat stiffly erect, as though conscious that it was considered divine, surveying the princess through unwinking green eyes that reminded her subtly of those of her father.

She had always despised the supercilious creature, but now, under its glare she began to experience a nervous fear. It seemed to have a sinister intelligence and to be mocking her. The idea came that it might really be supernatural, as the people believed—that it embodied some fiend or perhaps her father's Ka, that twin soul which Egyptians were supposed to possess. But her life on Mars had taught her to laugh at such superstitions, so she finally refused to think further along that line.

In the afternoon she watched while, to a great blare of trumpets, the Pharaoh, Refo and three adjutants drove out of the palace courtyard. They were preceded, as was the custom, by a pet leopard led by two Nubians. And they were surrounded by the guard of honor which would escort them to the city walls on their 600-league expedition.

Night came and with it a slave bearing two golden trays. On one reposed a generous slice of raw steak for Horus. On the other was the well-remembered jeweled cup of tepid water and decrepit piece of black bread.

She hurled the trays at the eunuch who brought them, then, as the door slammed on his dripping fat face, wished she hadn't, for the pangs of hunger had become insistent. She even thought of purloining the cat's meat from the floor, but Horus already had wolfed it down, and the bread with it.

Pan Doh Ra fell into fitful sleep intermingled with dreams of the horror which would descend upon Atlan if her father succeeded in his purpose. Half-waking she cursed the generous Martian strain in her which had prevented her killing the human monster. Fully awake, she shivered to note that the green eyes of the golden cat still were fixed unwinkingly upon her.

Dawn came and another weary, endless day. The conspirators must be far on their way by now. Computing the mileage as best she could, the princess reasoned that they would reach their destination in a week to ten days.

In a fury she again tugged at the unyielding bars. Then she vented her impotence by hurling bric-a-brac at the cat which unaccountably had changed its attitude and now insisted on fawning about her knees and striving to cover her with caresses. The animal dodged her missiles. After the barrage he retired to his corner, however, and bothered her no more.

It was the night of the fourth day. Pan Doh Ra could not sleep. For hours she crouched on a window seat, staring downward at the pinheads of light which set off Sais from the plain, and panting in the dead heat which presaged a sandstorm.

Suddenly there came a rush of air outside the window. Had the storm broken? She glanced upward, but stars still glittered in the black sky.

Again came the roar of wind, to die away as quickly as it came. But this time a great bulk screened the stars for an instant.

Pan Doh Ra's breath caught in her throat. Was it? Could it be? She pressed her face against the bars. Outside poised a great bat-winged creature which stared at her with beady, brilliant eyes.

"Sonny!" the girl called softly. "Sonny boy! To me!" she started the faint crooning at which she was so adept.

The 'dactyl balanced a moment. Catching her scent and the crooning, it slid suddenly downwind and clutched the bars with its murderous claws. Sobbing with delight that one friend still remembered her, Pan Doh Ra stroked the long, ludicrous head and whispered baby talk into the mousy ears.

Then a great thought struck her. "Sonny," she commanded. "Get me out of here. Come on, boy. Use that long head of yours."

The beast blinked sagely but made no move. Desperately she began to tug at the bars.

With a guttural cluck of understanding, Sonny hurled himself backward with a roar of wings, still clinging tightly to his perch.

Two of the iron bars snapped like dry sticks.

At this the cat, which had been bristling and spitting, screamed and launched itself full at the girl's breast, clawing at her eyes as she threw up frantic hands to protect her throat. The thing must have weighed twenty pounds and its attack forced her back against the broken bars until she was teetering over the void.

A demon seemed to possess Horus. He scratched her savagely, his hind legs ripping away the front of her gown. The pain became unbearable; the girl felt herself fainting as she strove vainly to grip the furry throat.

As she swayed through the window her back suddenly touched the pterodactyl's leathery skin. A long, snake-like neck shot over her shoulder. Cruel jaws clamped upon the back of the cat. Horus was jerked between the bars, shaken like a rat and hurled yowling into the night.

Sobbing with the weakness of reaction, Pan Doh Ra wriggled through the wrecked window. Somehow she got astride of Sonny's back and, gripping the loose skin between his wings, gave the command to rise.

The tropical moon was casting a mellow glow over the city as they swept around the palace to the accompaniment of a great shouting. Perhaps it was thought that Teraf had returned; perhaps the guard realized that the royal prisoner was escaping. However it was, there broke forth much snapping of guns and hurling of spears.

"Come on, rascal," shouted Pan Doh Ra as the long wings rose and fell, unharmed by the attack. "We're going to the Pillars of Heracles."

Chapter 16

. . . there occurred violent earthquakes and floods; and in a single day and night of misfortune all your warlike men in a body sank into the earth, and the island of Atlantis in like manner disappeared, and was sunk beneath the sea. PLATO's *Timaeus.*

Seven days out of Atlan, Teraf was encountering delays and heartbreaking difficulties. The roads in this almost unsettled part of the empire were atrocious. Fuel was hard to find; again and again he was forced to bump over long detours, or face the lengthy scrutiny of petty frontier officials.

Once in the Sicilian mountains his progress had been blocked by a lordly sabertooth. But the tawny monster decided at the last moment not to contest the passage of this evil-smelling metal intruder. After baring its foot-long fangs, it stepped proudly aside into the underbrush lining the excuse for a road.

Farther on, the Hellene had a brush with bandits who were taking advantage of the disorganization of communication to raid frontier towns.

It was in the Iberian village of Alhaba, nine days out, that the abused car expired. Careful inspection convinced Teraf that it was beyond repair by the local blacksmith. Moreover, the road leading west was a mere trail.

Leaving the machine to the mercies of the villagers, Teraf hurried to an inn on the shabby public square, displayed the seal of Atlan to the landlord and demanded a fast horse. That fat and greasy individual surveyed the sacred symbol indifferently, rang one of the gold coins which his visitor proffered and opined that it was false. Despite the fact that several good horses were stamping in the courtyard, he advised the Hellene to look elsewhere.

Crossing the square, Teraf interviewed the owner of the town's only other hostelry and was snubbed with equal abruptness.

As he turned to leave, the innkeeper's slatternly wife entered from a back room. On her dirty wrist was a wide gold bracelet bearing the Ibis crest.

"Where did you get that?" Teraf gripped her plump arm.

She whimpered, her eyes flickering toward her husband.

Instinctively the prince ducked, just in time to avoid a thrown bottle.

Before the dour Iberian could continue the barrage, Teraf's sword was out and he had pinned the man in a corner, with point at throat. "Where did she get it?" he snarled.

"Two men. . . . Please sir, don't kill your servant . . . They passed through here yesterday . . . The bracelet was a gift . . . to hinder those who followed."

Teraf's pulse throbbed in his temples. He dragged the quaking innkeeper into the courtyard and forced him to saddle and bridle the best of the horses. Then, after tossing several gold pieces on the ground he spurred out of town along the trail leading west.

The going became harder with each mile. It began to rain, a slow drizzle which soaked him to the bone. The country was wild and desolate; jagged rocks flanked the slippery road and sloped up to angry mountains which had their heads wrapped in mist.

He made twenty leagues before his horse foundered. This time he was able to obtain only a sorry nag from a farmer, but he kept on through the night.

At dawn he thought he sighted the figures of two horsemen at the top of a long rise far ahead. But they were gone behind a sheet of rain before he could be sure.

The Egyptains must have realized that they were being followed, for the next village turned out against Teraf with pitchforks, shovels and axes. He barely escaped with his life and lost many precious hours making a detour through swampy country.

It was on the morning of the second day after this that he caught sight of the massive Rock of Gibraltar rearing its head into the clearing skies. The white marble pyramid which served as the African buttress for Heracles' masterpiece still lay hidden in the mists, but the granite dam loomed across the entrance to the Mediterranean Valley. Behind it, he knew, raged the ever-rising Atlantic Ocean.

An hour before Teraf's arrival, the horsemen ahead of him had swept up the long ramp which led to the entrance of the pyramid and shouted for the guard.

In due time a sentry came out of his little box, yawning and dragging his gun behind him. Discipline had relaxed since the dam had been cut off from the rest of the world by the destruction of Bab El. He fell, his head burned off by a shot from the taller of the newcomers.

Both men then dismounted and unloosed a heavy object from one of the saddles. Before the startled commandant could leave his breakfast, they had gained the top of the pyramid, a flat lookout post surrounded by a low railing.

Puffing with apoplectic rage, the commandant stormed up the stairs with the rest of a now thoroughly-aroused guard at his back. He found his visitors standing at the edge of the platfrom, their backs to the thunderous Atlantic. They had placed their burden between them and were regarding him warily as he popped through a trap door.

"This is an outrage," stormed the fellow as he wiped egg from the corners of his pouting mouth. "You're under arrest." He struck an attitude.

Before the soldiers could move, Plu Toh Ra tossed an object about the size of a hand granade over the edge of the platform.

"Look!" he roared.

The missile struck the broad top of the dam and exploded in a flare of prismatic light. A section of the stone caught fire, blazed like pine for a moment, then vanished utterly. It left a hole in the top of the dam at which the ocean waves leaped hungrily.

"We are your Pharaoh," the voice boomed again. "That was merely a toy. At our feet is a bomb thousands of times more powerful. Bow down, if you wish to save the dam and your wretched lives."

"But—!" gabbled the commandant.

"But us no buts, slave. Aha, another of our pretty phrases! Bow down!"

The commandant bowed! Then he scuttled away, shooing before him those of the guard who had not already fled.

"Now what?" asked Refo. The triumph of which he had dreamed for years, and which had come so easily, tasted flat in his mouth. "We've captured the Pillars, all right, but we stand to starve to death up here, unless your armies reach here before those of Atlan."

The Pharaoh did not answer. He was pacing the platform, his hawk face lifted toward the hurrying, broken clouds, as he muttered prayers of thanksgiving to Isis, Osiris and the rest of his loathsome gods.

As though a bandage had been removed from his eyes, Refo saw—now that it was too late—that Plu Toh Ra was not the superman he had worshipped since his youth. This was merely a beak-faced, heartless barbarian who itched for power with which to aggrandize himself and his priests.

He tried to comfort himself with the thought that soon his Hellenes could return to the freedom of their Golden Age. At the same time he recalled the privation which had descended when the factories had stopped. What if there never had been a Golden Age?

The Pharaoh finally ceased his devotions and looked at Refo as though he had been a stranger. "You still here?" he growled at last. "Begone, Alfha traitor. Only Egypt must be found holding the dam when our minions arrive."

"What?" For a moment the Hellene's mind refused to grasp the significance of those words. "Very well," he resumed levelly after a long moment. "I will go. But let me warn you, Pharaoh, that when the commandant recovers from his fright he will realize that you don't dare destroy the dam because you also would be destroyed. Then he will come back with a hundred guards behind him. . . . You must be mad to think you can defend this platform alone."

"Mad? Who calls us mad?" screamed the Egyptian. "Begone, we say. We know you now. You're an Atlantean spy, trying to rob us of our empire. Isis! Osiris! Protect us!" He scrabbled in his garments for a weapon.

Clear and cold as a knifeblade, the realization came to Refo that he was facing a man gone insane. The attainment of Plu Toh Ra's ambition had tilted still farther a mind long distorted by passion, vice and religious frenzy.

"Come, friend," he pleaded, trying to bring the other back to reason. "You cannot succeed if you defy Atlantis alone. We must stand together. The battle is just beginning. Let us talk it over."

"Talk it over? With a spy?" bellowed the madman. "Defy the Atlanteans? Ho! Who said there would be any Atlanteans to defy?" He burst into a howl of laughter.

Then, quick as one of his sacred cats, the Pharaoh leaped toward the orichalcum bomb and started dragging its heavy container to the edge of the platform.

With a prayer on his lips, Refo hurled himself at the Egyptian, but the lead box was teetering on the edge of the pyramid nearest the sea before he could break the madman's grip on its handles.

With a grunt, Plu Toh Ra came erect. Refo did not give him time to reach for gun or dagger, but bored in with right and left jabs to the face and body. They grappled in the center of the platform. As they strained and heaved, the Greek realized, as he felt a rib crack, that he was no match for his giant antagonist. The muscles of the frenzied man seemed made of steel.

An old wrestling trick came to him. He drove his knee into the Egyptian's groin and leaped free as Plu Toh Ra screamed in agony.

But it gained only a momentary respite. Eyes blazing, the Pharaoh came in again, arms extended for a bone-crushing grip.

Refo lost a precious second in reaching for his knife and the other was upon him. Those tree-like arms locked once more about his middle. They fell together, managing by some miracle not to roll under the railing.

Back and forth they heaved and writhed. Refo had a slight advantage now, for the Egyptian was spending part of his energies trying to reach the bomb.

But the struggle was telling rapidly upon the Hellene. He was blinded with blood from a cut on his forehead, there came a roaring in his ears; he seemed to be breathing fire.

As his opponent weakened, Plu Toh Ra wriggled nearer and nearer the deadly box. At last he reached it with the toe of his sandal.

The bomb teetered sickeningly. Holding his foe with one hand now, the Pharaoh pushed again. The container scraped faintly on the marble, hesitated—then vanished over the edge.

The maniac was filled with wild delight. "Ho, proud Atlan," he gabbled, relaxing his hold somewhat on his victim. "Ho, nation of drowning rats. Ho, Refo, behold your empire. After us the deluge! Aha, a pretty phrase. Take it down, scribe!"

His old habit still working its customary reaction on a deranged mind, he glanced around for someone to write down his deathless words.

Realizing his opportunity, Refo rallied all his forces. Tearing one hand free, he snatched the Egyptian's dagger from its sheath and drove it deep under the ribs. Momentarily he noted how brightly the blood stained those barbaric vestments.

Plu Toh Ra lunged to his feet, dragging the other with him. His eyes looked into those of the Hellene and Refo saw that, somehow, those eyes had returned momentarily to sanity—that the events just passed had been forgotten.

"Ah, Hellene, you have betrayed us after all," whispered the wounded man. "We should have known better than to trust an Alfha with our dreams."

He clapped a hand to his wet side, withdrew it and stared, bemused, at the stain. His knees sagged. With a desperate effort he drew himself to his full height.

"We shall die together, then," he remarked simply.

Gripping Refo tightly, he hurled himself over the railing of the pyramid.

Chapter 17

This refilling of the Mediterranean . . . knew no check; it came, faster and faster; it rose over the tree tops, over the hills, until it had filled the whole basin of the Mediterranean and until it lapped the mountain cliffs of Arabia and Africa. Far away, long before the dawn of history, this catastrophe occurred. H. G. WELLS, *Outline of History*.

Teraf galloped up to the bottom of the pyramid just in time to see the dam guard scuttle out like rats and to witness the last moments of that fight on the platform. He divined from the actions of the tiny figures far above that something had changed his brother—that he was at last fighting on the side of Atlan and civilization.

For a time the combatants disappeared. Then came the climax, when Plu Toh Ra hurled himself and his enemy over the railing.

Down—down they shot together on their 1,000 foot slide over the steep marble slope toward the ground.

Teraf ran forward, pistol in hand, determined to finish the Egyptian at all costs if he lived through the descent. But, as they swept closer, he saw that the Pharaoh was on the bottom, his arms and legs flailing limply. Refo was clinging to the giant's chest as though trying to escape the rough spots.

When they were half way down the incline, however, there burst into the zenith from behind the wall a blaze of colors like ten thousand rainbows or an aurora borealis gone insane. This was accompanied by a roar as if all the fires of hell were burning together and followed by the telltale mushrooming cloud of a radioactive explosion.

Teraf was hurled to the ground and knocked senseless. When he recovered consciousness it was to find that his brother and the Egyptian had fallen only a few yards away.

Painfully he crawled forward and bent over them. Plu Toh Ra was quite dead and horribly mutilated. Refo still breathed, his arms locked about the neck of his late antagonist in a vice-like grip.

As the younger brother succeeded in separating the two, a

sound like thunder called his attention to the bulging center of the dam. A long crack appeared near the top of the structure. Stone spouted outward, impelled by the pressure behind it. Sea water followed in a roaring spout which melted the remaining stone like sugar and formed a pool which spread over the ground with lightning rapidity. In moments it blocked any hope of escape across the plain.

Working desperately against time, Teraf hoisted Refo on his shoulders and bound him there with strips from the Egyptian's torn garments. Then he took the only road to temporary safety. Balancing the unconscious man on his back he started a laborious climb up a series of handholds which had been cemented into the side of the pyramid. In a kind of frenzy he advanced under the deadweight burden. Up and up! Can't turn back! Must keep going!

The dam was dissolving before his staring eyes, but as yet the pyramid itself held firm. Boiling water was spreading in every direction below him and already lapping at the base of the tower. Dense clouds of steam formed but were whipped away by a rising wind.

Up, up and still up! His arms seemed torn from their sockets. His hands and knees were bleeding and torn. Every rung in the ladder was a new achievement and a new agony.

He dared look down no longer; the slope was too steep for that. Was the flood gaining on him? Out of the corner of his eye he saw another section of the dam give way. The roar of waters deafened him and made his senses reel.

Once he missed a chiseled niche and swung dizzily by one hand while a crazy world spun beneath him. Hours later, it seemed, he dragged himself and his burden over the edge of the bloodstained platform.

"Now what?" he wondered.

The answer was—death. There could be no escape. On three sides the pyramid breasted a whirlpool. On the fourth—the one which had connected it with the heights of the African shore—a great crack had developed, through which a scythe of water was slashing. Almost all of the dam had disappeared by now, to be replaced by a foaming chute of liquid, eight miles wide and moving with the speed of a dream.

Inland the water had spread out and was sweeping forward in a solid sheet, crested with uprooted trees and even solid blocks from the dam. Already it had inundated the countryside for several miles and was plunging on toward the horizon.

Teraf stood up shakily and looked about him. A mile to the

north he saw the craven commandant and his soldiers overtaken and swept away like ants before the stream from a hose. They had foolishly attempted to reach the Iberian cliffs instead of the African heights.

Now the pyramid itself began trembling from the onrush of the ocean. Massive almost beyond belief, it still tilted ever so slightly as its foundations were undermined. In a matter of minutes it, too, would begin to dissolve.

As Teraf tried to remember forgotten boyhood prayers to Gaea and Chronus, a movement by Refo caused him to forget them and kneel quickly.

The elder Hellene's eyelids flickered. Lifting his head, he caught the significance of the mad scene and burst into wracking sobs.

"I've been a fool and a traitor, Teraf," he gasped. The latter had to put his ear close to the moving lips to catch the words.

"I ask no forgiveness," Refo went on, his voice gathering force. "I committed the unpardonable sin—the sin against all mankind. I was just a boy when I first met Plu Toh Ra, shortly after you went to Mars. He painted . . . pictures. He told of the woes of our peoples . . . imaginary woes, mostly, I know now. But at that time I was a knight errant, and besides, I loved a princess. My eyes were blinded by the Pharaoh's personality, too. Instead of looking about me, I believed everything he said and joined in his high quest."

He reached out a bloodstained claw and grasped the equally damaged hand of his brother.

"All this," he muttered. "May I be forever accursed. May a vulture peck at my vitals forevermore. I thought to bring light to my people. Instead I brought death to a world."

His eyes fluttered shut. As the pyramid lurched and swayed, threatening at every moment to hurl them into the abyss, Teraf waited with bated breath, the tears streaming down his face.

But Refo was not dead. His eyes opened again. For a moment he stared vacantly, then struggled to a sitting position.

"Look!" he screamed, his eyes almost starting from their sockets. "We are saved!"

Wondering what fevered image his brother had glimpsed, Teraf glanced upward. Then he too shouted and leaped to his feet in an ecstasy of wonder.

Sweeping down toward them through the tempest, descending in long, slow spirals, came a pterodactyl. From between its wings peered the white face of Pan Doh Ra.

Sonny plainly had no desire to land on the rocking platform. But the girl belabored him with her fist, choked him, finally prodded him with her dagger. At last the reptile chose the lesser of two evils and came in for a two point landing.

"Quick," shrilled its rider as the beast clung to the railing, facing the storm and flattening its wings against the floor in order not to have them torn away. "Sling Refo across his back. There! Now get on behind him. Sonny can carry three with this wind behind him. Quick! If you love me, quick! The pyramid is sinking."

Toiling like one possessed, Teraf lifted his brother into position and bound him there as best he could. Then he gripped loose folds of skin on the bony back and mounted, while the monster eyed him wrathfully.

"Up, Sonny boy," crooned Pan Doh Ra, bending over the snake-like neck. "Up with you if you don't want to get your fur wet."

The 'dactyl flapped its wings obligingly, but did not rise. The load was too great.

"Leave me behind," Refo begged, struggling with his bonds. "Let me die here. That will save Zeus the trouble of executing me."

"Up, lazy beast," the girl shouted, but to no purpose.

The problem was solved for them at that moment. Slowly, but with definite purpose, the pyramid began to settle on its side. The sea rose toward them, its waves reaching out like hungry maws.

The pterodactyl squealed with terror, its wings flapped madly. As the platform fell from under them, it caught a rush of wind and rose sluggishly into the stormy air.

Chapter 18

I sprang to the stirrup, and Joris and he;
I galloped, Dirck galloped, we galloped all three;

Behind shut the postern, the lights sank to rest
And into the midnight we galloped abreast.

ROBERT BROWNING.

The flight was a nightmare of roaring winds and black skies. Their reptile seemed to creep over the landscape although, in reality it was making a steady seventy-five miles an hour flying before the gale which had risen to aid the flood waters in their terrible work.

"Think we'll make it?" Teraf shouted once to Pan Doh Ra who, with black hair flying, was riding the neck of her steed like a Valkyrie.

"If Sonny's strength holds. I don't dare land to rest him, for he would never go up again with the three of us. If he keeps going we should be there before dawn. Can we beat the ocean, though?"

"Oh yes. The water must spread over the entire valley as it comes. We should be a day or two in advance of it, at least. See. Already we've drawn ahead.

He pointed downward, where unbroken forests were bowing to the storm. Far to the rear, a white wall of water pursued them. As they watched, it took a village in its stride. They saw a few peasants run aimlessly across the plain to be obliterated by the torrent. Teraf only imagined that he heard their screams.

Throughout the night, which was unlit by moon or star, they flapped onward.

"Sonny has the homing instinct," the girl said once. "He'll head for Sais. That should take us within sight of Atlan."

Refo recovered sufficiently to sit up. The three clung together, shivering with the cold, soaked by the driving rain, yet nodding now and then from sheer exhaustion.

The elder Hellene was a broken man. His mind wandered. Alternately he cursed Plu Toh Ra and himself for having brought on the debacle. Finally he slept, his arms about the princess, his head on her shoulder, while Teraf supported him from the rear.

"Not a bad sort, your brother," the girl called over her shoulder. "If only he could learn to laugh. Life gets tangled up if one goes through it with a long face. You should never have left him, Teraf. He was no match for the Pharaoh.

"Poor father," she went on sadly. "If mother had lived, he would have been different, I think. She could laugh at him and make his illusions of grandeur seem ridiculous. I tried that, too, after she was gone, but I was only a little girl. For the want of a laugh, an empire was lost. Plu Toh Ra would have loved that phrase—would have had it inscribed on papyrus or marble. How he did adore those trite phrases. . . . Honestly thought he invented them. When I told him they were as old as the Nile he beat me."

"You loved him, then?" Teraf was frankly puzzled.

"Why yes, I guess I did, in a way. He was all I had after mother died. If Zeus hadn't been a dear, softhearted old fool he would have disciplined my Pharaoh years ago. That would have put an end to his ambitions. When I was a child, before the high priest began to whisper in his ear, he wasn't so bad. Let that be his epitaph."

She was silent, while Sonny's wings flapped above and below them with monotonous regularity. Teraf touched her shoulder. "May I laugh with you, if we get out of this?"

She reached back and squeezed his hand.

Dawn came, a ragged whitening of the sullen clouds. With it, Sonny seemed to lose the mechanical smoothness of his flight. The rhythm of his wing-stroke faltered again and again. But under the admonishments of Pan Doh Ra he always managed to pick up the swing, as though he realized that heroic efforts were expected of him. Now and then he whimpered, however, and turned his hideous head back to stare at his mistress with red-rimmed eyes.

"We'd better lighten ship," said the princess at last. "I should have thought of it before."

She kicked off her sandals and tore from her throat and wrists the priceless necklaces and bracelets which adorned them, tossing the jewels away without a sigh.

Teraf, and Refo, who had awakened by now, followed her example by casting away their weapons and shoes.

Sonny squealed as if in appreciation. The beat of his wings steadied.

It was three o'clock that afternoon before the crooked mountain surmounting Atlan was revealed to them by a ray of sunlight which flashed providentially through a break in the clouds.

"Hurrah! We're making it," shouted the girl.

The cry seemed to rattle the pterodactyl. It winced and turned glazed eyes toward them. The beat stopped. The black wings shot upward. They were falling like a plummet.

"He's gone," said Pan. The beast's head was flopping loosely. "Goodbye Teraf. Goodbye Refo. I've tried . . ."

Then, as the ground whirled up to meet them, Sonny made his last effort. His bat wings started their beat again. He pulled up several hundred feet from the ground and went on.

The princess screamed with joy. To lighten the burden still further she tore off her already scanty garments and rode before them, naked as dawn. Refo and Teraf followed her example.

For a few minutes the wings steadied to almost their old, tireless swing. Atlan, beautiful in its groves, its marble porticoes and blue, encircling canals, came swiftly nearer. Teraf saw that the streets were decorated with flags and filled with people.

Pan spoke to her steed then, starting him on a long glide toward the palace grounds. Wild with excitement, she turned and, over Refo's shoulder, kissed Teraf full on the lips.

"We'll save them yet," she cried. "Given two days, they can escape to the highlands of Crete and Sicily or build makeshift boats and float to safety."

But something was wrong with Sonny again. Wings stiffly extended but his great head sagging, he quivered and jerked so that his riders had to cling tightly. Lower and lower he swept in a straight, steep glide. Teraf could see the upturned faces of the crowds below and the guns of the fortress swinging to bear on them.

The princess pleaded wildly with her mount, beat him with her fists, prodded with the dagger. There was no response. The glide continued.

"We'll miss the palace," she cried. "We're falling into a canal," she screamed a second later.

The inner band of water, its bridges lined with watchers, caromed toward them. They were so close that Teraf could see the open-mouthed wonder on the faces. . . .

They struck with a terrific splash. One of the wings crumpled back, wrapping Teraf in its rubbery folds. The waters closed over his head. He struggled desperately for a moment, then relaxed. It was too much trouble. He was tired.

Chapter 19

Which removeth the mountains, and they know not; which overturneth them in his anger.
Which shaketh the earth out of her place and the pillars thereof tremble. *Job,* 8-5 and 6.

"Great Land of Nod!" Teraf heard the words as he pitched and rolled on a red hot gridiron in hell. "He's coming 'round after all."

The Hellene opened his eyes and stared blankly—at the ground. The agony continued. He turned his head to discover Hermes kneeling across his body, pumping firmly on his ribs.

Water poured from his nose and mouth. He spluttered and fought. At that Hermes released him and rolled him over.

"Wh—what you trying to do?" Teraf gasped like a fish. Then, as memory returned, "Where are the others?"

"They're safe, up at the palace." The chronicler was all grins. "Knocked out cold by the crash but coming around. Had the devil's own time dragging you from under that carcass. Thought you were done for." He mopped his perspiring face and leaned weakly against a buttress of the nearby bridge.

Someone threw a robe over Teraf's nakedness. He sat up, blinking at the throng of blurred faces about him. The faces started spinning and blacked out.

"Easy now," he heard Hermes saying. "Lie down and take it easy. I'll get a stretcher and carry you to the palace. A good sleep should bring you 'round all right."

"Sleep!" The horror of what impended cleared the prince's head. He dragged himself to his feet. "The flood is coming. Heracles' dam has been smashed. Take me to the Pitar at once."

Instantly he realized his mistake. After a frozen moment the faces about him paled. Then there was a puzzled muttering which broke into frenzied shouts.

"The dam! The dam is out!" screamed an Alfha who was first to understand the implication. "Flee for your lives! The ocean is coming."

The shout was taken up by others. The crowd milled about, then started racing across the bridge in blind panic. Screams rent the air. Within seconds, people were being pushed over the balustrades by the crush.

Teraf's knees buckled, but Hermes slipped an arm around his shoulders and held him up. Together they started running toward the palaces, which lay a quarter of a mile through the park. As they went the strength of despair flowed into the Hellene and lent wings to his feet.

"What are the flags and crowds for?" he managed to gasp as they raced up a broad driveway.

"Bab El— Been repaired. Power goes on in an hour. Feast Day. All that."

"Too late."

"I know. But what a scoop this is for the *Planet*. . . . The last scoop. Hey there, king, watch out for the tree. That's it. This way."

They stumbled up a flight of steps, through the reception hall, burst past the guards before the audience chamber door and literally fell into the presence of the monarch, who was holding a consultation with Athena and Heracles.

Athena screamed at the sight. Heracles leaped forward and caught the messenger of doom as he slumped.

Word by word, Teraf panted out his story while Hermes, despite the fact that his wound was not completely healed, sprinted for the vision screen to get his last scoop to the *Planet.*

". . . have at most two days," the Hellene concluded.

The Pitar's copper-colored face had turned almost white at the news. Tearing Hermes away from the visor in the midst of his story, Zeus spun the dials until Hephaestus' face appeared on the screen.

"Turn the power on immediately," he thundered. "Damn the danger" (as the engineer began to protest). "Turn on the power instantly. The dam has been broken and the flood is coming."

Ares was called next. The Pitar shot him close-clipped orders to make ready the flying fleet, load the ships with refugees as rapidly as possible and unload at Crete. "Come back and load again," he concluded. "Keep it up till your men drop."

"Can't save a tithe of them now," the warlord barked. "City's in an uproar already. Streets jammed. Panic. Do best we can."

"Cut in the public screens as soon as the power comes on, then. Warn everybody to make for the mountains. Take any other measures necessary," Zeus was continuing when an imperative screaming from the machine caused him to make rapid adjustments.

"The power's on," he cried over his shoulder. "I'll try to reach Sicily."

There was a nerve-wracking delay, but at last the scared face of the Sicilian commandant appeared.

"Yes," he babbled. "The water's almost here. It will be pouring through the valleys within a few hours. We're evacuating to the mountains. Some may escape."

The Pitar whirled.

"It's coming faster than we thought," he snapped. "We don't have much more than twenty-four hours. Athena, take over here and warn your colonies. The entire valley is doomed, tell them. Only the mountains offer safety. Tell them the power's on and to use every means of transport . . . build rafts . . . anything.

"Heracles," he shouted at the engineer, who had been sobbing windily. "Stop that blubbering. Get down to the military section and help Ares.

"Hermes, you may have the screen when Athena finishes.

Tell your paper to issue extras and handbills showing the best routes to the highlands if it can get anybody to man the presses. If it can't, go down and man them yourself.

"Teraf, help Hermes if you are able. If not, report to Dr. Vanya."

Hermes looked at Athena for a moment, then shook his head and turned toward the door. As Teraf started to follow him to the *Planet* offices, Zeus slipped an arm about his shoulders.

"Good work, my boy," he said sadly. "No one could have done more. You say your brother has redeemed himself somewhat. I'm glad. Always did say he was a good man gone wrong. I'll put him to work if he recovers. Drop in and see your princess before you go into the city. Better get some clothes, too."

It was only then that Teraf realized he was still clad only in a cloak. One of the guards brought him his harness and he slipped into it before hurrying to the infirmary.

"I'm glad! I'm glad!" Pan Doh Ra sobbed incoherently as she clung to him. "Oh, Teraf. You're all right. I love you. Poor Sonny. Is Refo all right? Half my own people will drown in the lowlands of the Nile. Have I done enough to atone for the Pharaoh's sin? I love you." She was rapidly becoming hysterical.

Disregarding a hovering nurse, he shook her roughly and managed to restore her composure. But now a new problem presented itself. Disregarding the objections of her nurse, and merely laughing when she caught sight of her bandaged head in a mirror, the girl got out of bed and announced that she did not intend to leave her lover.

It was useless to argue.

"Where you go, I go," she declared. "I'll never let you out of my sight again. You always get into trouble when I do. If we die tomorrow, we'll at least die together." Taking his arm, she led him out of the room.

At the vantage point of the palace facade they halted for a moment to stare out over the city. Its streets were black with people. A faint clamor of shouting rose from the crowds.

Already the suburban plains were alive with fugitives. Radio cars drove madly through unfortunates fleeing on foot. The dread which had overhung Atlan ever since the oceans had started their slow rise a century before had left no room for doubt of the catastrophe, once the rumor had spread.

As they watched, the first airships, laden to the rails, took off from the military circle, skimmed over the city and headed for Crete.

"Tens of thousands will be saved," whispered Teraf as he guided his sweetheart into the repulsion car reserved for use on royal command.

"And millions will die." Her tired face was wet with tears.

Chapter 20

A land of darkness, as darkness itself; and of the shadow of death, without any order, and where the light is as darkness. *Job,* 10-22.

The car took them through the military sector, but the bridges across the second canal into the city proper were jammed with wild-eyed humanity. They had to fight the rest of their way on foot.

Under the stress of the panic, Atlan's police system had broken down. Here and there frantic patrolmen, in their distinctive green trappings, struggled vainly to keep the crowds in some sort of order. Teraf saw one officer stop in the midst of an impassioned harangue, throw up his arms and begin screaming. He had been caught, like millions of others, in the universal hysteria.

A few barbarians who could not grasp the impending disaster, were looting deserted warehouses as they passed through the second circle. They eyed Pan Doh Ra's dark beauty like buyers at a slave mart, but drew back when Teraf placed a hand on his pistol.

Weary from battling the mobs which fought to storm the hangars and the even greater throngs which—carrying what few belongings they could salvage—were heading for the suburbs, Teraf and the girl staggered at last through the Planet Building's imposing portals. They found the offices seething with hysterical but well-directed activity. The presses were roaring with the final edition, an Extra printed entirely in red. Its headlines played down the disaster and implored the populace to "be calm." Inside were reassuring statements by government leaders, marked by maps of the best routes to safety.

Teraf located a sweating Hermes who dragged them into the broadcasting studios and put them to work with a group of superficially calm young men whose duty it was to do their utmost to quiet the panic. For hours they begged the unheeding masses of humanity on the streets to build rafts, and made impossible promises of rescue for all.

As the sun went down and the evening passed with sickening rapidity the staff began to dwindle as here and there reporters rose from their work, glanced guiltily about and hurried out.

Seeing this, Nubro, the *Planet's* editor, began wandering about the offices, soothing his men, dropping words of advice and cracking jokes. Many a young reporter with fear-whitened lips took a new grip on himself as he felt the great man's hand on his shoulder and turned back to continue his hoarse and useless shouting to the stampeding crowds.

But Nubro could not be everywhere at once. It was hardly midnight when he approached the three friends, gripped Hermes and Teraf by the hands and said, as though commenting on the weather, "You folks had better get back to the palace. The printing staff is entirely gone. I'll try to hold a few men to continue broadcasting until dawn. You can do nothing more here."

He escorted them to the door and waved a grim farewell as they dived into the mob.

The confusion was even worse than when they had come. There were now two struggling currents of refugees. One stream of hopeful figures was hurrying toward the military sector, confident of escape in the airships. An equal number, haggard from wasting precious hours at the jammed bridges, were fighting their way toward the open country.

Endless traffic jams and savage, reasonless fights were taking place. The bright streets, which that morning had been filled with merrymakers, were strewn with personal belongings and occasional battered bodies. Serene on the rooftops, an occasional skeptic watched the battle, confident in his ignorance that the flood could never come.

The bridges to the military sector were completely jammed by now. For blocks a packed mass of humanity screamed and begged to be allowed to cross. From time to time the heavy bridge gates were opened for a few seconds to allow several thousand lucky ones to enter, then crowded shut again by husky soldiers. To prevent anyone from swimming the canal and overpowering the military, fire screens had been turned partly on. Their lurid rays lent an unearthly glow to the mad scene.

For a time the exhausted trio tried to fight a way through the mob. It was no use. Those they tried to displace struck at them with fists or knives and held them at bay.

Hermes, his hand over his aching wound, at last sank to the ground.

"There's no way through that mob unless we can fly," he gasped. "Shall we head for the open country?"

"Might be a way under them," hazarded Teraf. "The catacombs—"

"The catacombs!" Hermes struggled to his feet. "What a super-idiot I am. Come on. Let's try them anyway. There's an entrance near here."

Under his guidance they entered a deserted warehouse, squeezed through a slit in the cellar wall and found themselves in a damp, bone-filled tunnel.

"I'm not sure," the chronicler hesitated. "I've been down here with a torch, but it's different in the dark. Come on, though. It's our only chance."

Joining hands, they crept along the passage. Again and again their feet crushed through ancient skeletons or they bumped painfully into rocks and beams fallen from the roof.

"There should be an exit about here if we took the right turning," Hermes muttered at last. "We should have passed under the canal. Where is that damned exit? My matches are all gone. We'll have to separate and feel along the walls. All of us must shout at intervals so we can keep in touch."

They followed his directions and wandered about, testing the mouldy walls with their hands, disturbing flights of bats, gasping in the putrid air. And all the while precious minutes were passing and unreasoning fear that the waters might come and drown them like rats in a burrow was growing upon them. At times Teraf had to bite his lips to keep from howling.

At first they kept close together, but as the chambers branched, were forced to separate farther and farther, still keeping in touch by shouts.

At last Teraf shouted Pan Doh Ra's name and got no answer.

"Pan! Pan!" he called again and again, but only the rustling of the wings of bats he had disturbed answered him.

A hand gripped his arm. It was that of Hermes, who had returned from an excursion into a dead-end tunnel.

"Which way was she when you last heard her?" he demanded.

"Straight ahead—I think."

"Come on, then."

For an infinity they cast about, shouting. When it seemed that all hope was lost, a faint hail responded to theirs. They ran forward, stumbling over rocks and phosphorescent bone piles.

"Pan!" shouted Teraf after a particularly mad scramble had left him bruised and bleeding.

"Here," answered the faraway ghost of a voice. "I've found a crack in the wall, I think. There's a draft coming in."

A few moments later she was in the Hellene's arms, shaking as with the ague. "I got lost," she sobbed. "Couldn't make you hear me. I must have fainted, I guess. When I came to, there was a faint breath of air fanning my face."

They explored frantically. Finally the chronicler gave vent to a shout of joy. "Here it is. We must have missed it by inches before. Follow me."

"Looks like rain," he panted inanely as they stood in the open shortly thereafter, filling their lungs in great gasps.

Indeed, lightning was flashing in the west. Huge banks of cloud, pierced through by forks of flame, were creeping rapidly toward the zenith.

They became conscious once more of the imploring voice of the populace from across the canal. In the glow of the fire screens, thousands of pale faces were turned toward the hangars near which they now stood. Those in the front rank stretched out imploring arms; mothers lifted babies so they might be seen. Occasionally the crush became so great that people were pushed into the canal, there to die in the boiling waters.

Turning away from that ghastly scene, the three found their way to the war lord. The great man was in his element as he stood, legs wide, hands behind back, in the midst of his officers, shouting laconic instructions regarding the loading of his ships.

"Not needed here," Ares grunted when they had managed to reach his side. "Job for the military." But as they turned to go he held up his hand imperiously. "One moment," he snapped. "Ship being withdrawn for use in rescuing those at palace. Help provision it."

Then he thawed for a moment and gripped the hand of each in turn. "Good luck. May not meet again. Appreciate your spirit." He jerked away and began shouting orders as before.

A subaltern led them to the appointed ship, a war cruiser capable of carrying 500 refugees. It left its moorings as the watching citizens screamed in disappointment. A short while later it descended on the plain surrounding Bab El Tower.

As they alighted, the storm broke in a downpour of rain and roar of shifting winds.

For hours they moved between the power station, the palace and the ship, carrying provisions, weapons, light machinery, important records and many lead orichalcum containers. Nothing was forgotten which would tend to make life easier for the exiles-to-be. Over their heads as they worked charged endless flights of ships going and coming from the military sector. Even the *Poseidon,* clumsy though she was for anything but interplanetary travel, had been pressed into service, they noted, and was carrying thousands to safety.

Despite the fact that she had not slept for days, Pan Doh Ra worked like a man, thrusting her streaming shoulders against bales of boxes, sometimes throwing herself down on the flooded ground for a brief rest, but always arising to join her lover.

"For the first time in my life I'm doing useful labor," she called out once. And again: "This is better than being a princess on bread and water."

As the blinding storm let up for an interval, Teraf realized that a man toiling beside him was Refo. The brothers gripped hands silently, then went stubbornly on with their work.

A bleak dawn was filtering through the clouds when Hephaestus, who had been supervising the preparations, reported that the ship could carry no more cargo and was ready to load passengers.

He called Teraf, Refo and Pan Doh Ra to him. Together they splashed down to the palace, entering the audience chamber to find Zeus still tinkering with the visor dial. Hera's plump body was occupying his throne. The pitaress, who usually went about in a fever of excitement, had become calm in the crisis and was speaking words of encouragement to her harassed spouse.

The ruler glanced at the newcomers through red-rimmed eyes, then turned back to the controls. "Been trying to get the commandant at Albia," he said over his shoulder. "Looks as if they had been flooded."

"But Albia is only a little more than forty leagues from Atlan," Hephaestus exploded. "If it is flooded we have only three or four more hours. It's time to get everyone aboard."

For a moment longer Zeus twisted the dials, then shrugged as he turned away from the useless machine.

Soon the cable cars which connected the palace with the top of Crooked Mountain were filled with the royal household, palace attendants, soldiers and officials. They came quietly, but all turned their faces, whenever possible, toward their former home.

The Pitar and his council were the last to go. The old man stood in the Bab El control room surveying those who had worked with him for so many decades—who had witnessed, most of them, the rise and fall of the greatest empire the world had ever known.

"We have done our best, friends," he said to them quietly. "I thank you. Of course our exile will be only temporary. Communications will be reestablished with Mars in a few months or years. Then Atlantis will grow mightier than before.

"Until then, we shall be forced to live in some region out of reach of the waters. I suggest the mountains of Hellas. Athena, do you approve?"

"That would be safest," his silvery-haired daughter nodded. "We should be able to establish ourselves there, now that Refo has rejoined us. The Hellenes like me. They will have, I believe, a wholesome respect for us if we use them fairly. Besides, since Hellas is the weakest spot in the empire except Egypt, we should settle there and try to revive their loyalty so that the glory of Atlantis may be more quickly revived if—when communications are restored."

"It certainly would be a good idea to have those shameless Hellenes where we could watch them," Hera burst out. "I always said . . ." Zeus shook his gray head and his wife subsided.

"Are we all here?" asked the Pitar. He glanced about the room, checking off those present.

"What of Aphrodite?" Hephaestus hesitated.

"By my crooked scepter, I had forgotten," Zeus admitted, shamefaced as though he had been caught in a major crime. "She is confined to her quarters. Apollo, go fetch her."

A few moments later the woman who had made the deluge possible entered the room. Unlike all the others, who were reeling with fatigue, she was carefully gowned and her gorgeous hair was bound with a silver fillet. But she was pale under her rouge and seemed smaller than when they had last seen her. And there were faint lines on the oval face.

"Kill me. Kill me," she moaned, kneeling at her father's feet and resting her head on the floor. "I am not fit to live."

Teraf, listening, detected the same theatrical note as of old. She was playing the martyr now, he thought, and his lips curled; the others drew back as though she might contaminate them. But Zeus gently lifted her up and slipped his arm around her shoulders. "Too late for that, my dear," he said.

Aphrodite heaved a fluttering sigh and threw her bare round arms about him. The Pitar's mood changed at the gesture; he shook her off brusquely and turned to give orders for the exodus.

The last council on the soil of Atlantis was held in that little office while, just outside, the black hulk of the warship gleamed in the downpour.

Hephaestus was the first speaker. Balancing on his crippled legs, he looked at everyone in turn and then said simply: "Two of us must stay here, Your Pitarship. The power machinery will go out of balance immediately if left to operate by itself. I shall stay, of course, but I need one assistant. He does not need to be an engineer. He will only have to pull levers and carry out my instructions. I would ask one of my own men to stay, but each of them has a family and I would not separate them. I would prefer an unmarried man."

"Who will volunteer?" asked Zeus.

Every person in the room stepped forward. Even Aphrodite, an hysterical light in her green eyes, begged permission to die in this heroic fashion. Heracles also was insistent.

Zeus shook his head at both of them. "No, Heracles. I will need your engineering knowledge in Hellas." Then, patting the hand of his daughter, he said, "Such a death would be too noble for you, my dear."

"What about me?" Hera startled them all by asking.

"The quiet simplicity of paradise would never suit your tastes. Besides, I would be helpless without you to care for me." The last words seemed to give him pause. "But my life is about over. Why shouldn't I stay?" He looked hard at Hephaestus. "Two old friends, dying together."

"If I can't stay, neither can you, sir," growled Heracles, flexing his muscles.

There was a movement in the tightly-packed group and Refo pushed his way forward. "It's not your duty but mine, Pitarship," he declared firmly. "All this could not have happened except for me. I must stay."

"So be it," said Zeus after a moment's thought. Then to the others. "Come. It's time to go."

Pan Doh Ra stepped forward, her dark hair gleaming wetly in the pale morning light. Behind her stood Teraf.

"One more request, Father Zeus," she smiled wanly. "I am Queen of Egypt now. I also am partially responsible for this—for this mess. I've been talking to Teraf. We agree that if you can lend us a small ship we'll go to Sais instead of Hellas and try to hold Egypt for the Empire. The Hellenes love and will obey Athena. You'll not need Teraf."

Again the Pitar considered, to nod at last.

"You're a smart girl, Pan." He pressed her hand. "My private ship, which holds two passengers only, is in the palace hangar. Take it, and God be with you." He motioned Teraf to advance and, almost bashfully, laid a hand on each of their heads in the old Pitaric blessing.

"Time's up," Hephaestus interrupted. "Two hours at most before the flood reaches Atlan, and possibly another two before it becomes deep enough to submerge the power station. You'd best go at once. When the station is wrecked, power will drain out of the ether like water through a sieve. Your ships will have time enough to land after that happens, but no more. If you go at once you may reach Hellas and Egypt."

Oppressed by a sadness greater than they had ever known, the little company filed by the crippled engineer and the tall, dark Hellene who now stood at his side, gripping their hands and saying a few inadequate words of farewell before passing out into the rain to be shepherded aboard ship by Mars and his lieutenants.

As Pan Doh Ra stepped forward, Refo dropped to his knees and, seizing her hands, covered them with kisses.

"I am beneath notice because I believed the worst of you," he whispered so softly that the others could not hear. "No, don't say you forgive me," as she opened her lips to object. "I'm not worth forgiveness. Only remember that I loved you even when I said I hated you. But Teraf cares for you more than I know how to. You will be happy together."

He rose, gripped his brother's arms for a moment, then fled into the interior of the station.

Chapter 21

And behold, there came a great wind from the wilderness and smote the four corners of the house, and it fell upon the young men, and they are dead: And I only am escaped to tell thee. *Job*, 10-19.

The rulers of Atlantis filed slowly into the streaming black ship which already housed all the other refugees from the inner circle.

Zeus was the last to go. For a long minute he stood staring out over his rain-washed empire. Atlan blazed with lights which were only partially dimmed by the illumination pouring out of the ship's open hatches. The cries of the city's inhabitants were muted by distance. From the military zone, laden ships were still departing for Crete as empty ones returned to assume new burdens.

At last the Pitar bowed his gray head, placed the tips of his fingers to his brow in the ancient Martian salute, then limped slowly up the nearest ramp. The door closed behind him with an irrevocable hiss of compressed air.

From the office, Teraf and Pan watched the hull rise lazily from its muddy resting place. At the altitude of 300 feet it circled the mountain, then turned toward the northeast. In seconds it was lost among the clouds.

"This is no time for weeping," the girl sobbed as she slipped cold fingers into her lover's hand. "They'll make Athens. We must be sure to reach Sais. Let's go."

They clambered into the cable car and dropped silently toward the shining palace. As they dashed through its echoing corridors, they were startled by a faint yapping from Aphrodite's chambers. Teraf pushed open the door. Inside crouched a little dog which was whimpering with loneliness and that uncanny foreknowledge of disaster which brutes have.

Scooping up the forgotten pet, the Hellene followed Pan Doh Ra toward the Pitar's roof hangar. There it took only a few moments to push the slim, cigar-shaped flier out on its runway and to squeeze into its little cabin. Soon they were circling above the city, the dog nestling contentedly under the girl's robe.

The seething crowds on the streets of Atlan looked like ants in a disturbed hill. The entire countryside also was alive with minute pedestrians—motorists long since had reached safety or deserted their mired vehicles. All the refugees were heading northward toward the mountains across fields which had been churned into quagmires.

Over this ghastly scene, airships continued to dash back and forth on their errands of mercy. The warlord would not stop them, they knew, until there was just time for the last passengers to reach safety.

With a stab of agony, Teraf recalled his first glimpse of Atlan when he had returned from Mars such a few weeks before. Except for the mob, the scene looked much the same. Then the street lights had been alight because of the gloom. Now they gleamed forgotten as they would do until the waters descended. Beacons were flashing as usual in the military circle. The marble buildings gleamed white in the endless rain.

"Won't we wake up soon and find that this is a dream—that everything is as it used to be?" breathed Pan. "Surely no flood can destroy all this power—all this beauty."

For answer Teraf turned the ship toward Egypt and gave it full power. As he did so there came a momentary rift in the clouds which allowed a warm shaft of sunlight to illuminate the city. They strained backward for a last glimpse of Atlan. Brave and clear as a cameo it lay, a gem on a strip of green velvet.

He heard the girl sobbing heartbrokenly.

The beam of sunlight passed on, swept westward. In the far distance it flashed across an endless white line which was advancing majestically toward the town.

The clouds closed again and the vision faded.

For two hours they flew, crossing the Egyptian frontier at last and rapidly approaching their destination. A half hour more would see them safely landed at Sais.

It was then that Pan Doh Ra, who had been weeping softly with her head on her lover's shoulder, looked up and made a discovery. There was a tiny vision screen on the ship's instrument board.

"There's a screen in the Bab El engine room," she exclaimed as she manipulated the visor dials. "I must try to tell Refo that I do forgive him. I'll never sleep again if I don't."

Several minutes passed without a response to their call. Then a blur of light appeared on their four-inch screen. It swirled, brightened and finally coalesced to show the Bab El control room.

Hephaestus and Refo were there, working furiously in water which reached to their ankles. In the background, generators and transformers purred smoothly.

"Refo!" cried the princess.

The Hellene looked up, lifted one hand to his forehead as he caught sight of her on his own screen, then hurried to help the hunchbacked engineer, who was frantically shifting dampers in the pile which occupied the rear wall of the room.

When this task was done, Refo turned back to the screen.

"Can you make it to Sais?" he inquired calmly.

"Yes," the two refugees spoke together. And Teraf added through dry lips, "We're only about twenty leagues away, now."

"Good." Refo might have been talking about the weather. "The city is gone—tidal wave hit it half an hour ago." He staggered as the engineroom door burst open and the water about him gushed higher.

"When you feel the power weaken, go into a steep glide," interrupted Hephaestus. Having completed his last act as engineer of Bab El, he waded forward and now stood beside his helper, mopping his bald head. "That way you should be able to land before the ether drains."

"Can't you still get away?" cried Teraf in a sudden frenzy as he recalled what he had forgotten before—that a two-place flier was always kept at the top of Crooked Mountain.

The cripple shrugged as he leaped to a switchboard to make an adjustment.

"The pile would blow in two minutes if left to itself," he replied stoically. "The military ships are still in the air on their last flight and the Pitar's party hasn't landed yet. We're in for it. Good luck to you. Remember about that glide." He stumbled away through the hip-deep flood.

"Refo!" screamed Pan Doh Ra as the Hellene turned to follow. "Listen! I do forgive you. Goodbye. God keep you."

The face of the man in the engine room lighted. He sloshed forward as though trying to touch her. His face magnified until it filled the tiny screen.

"Thank you, my love," he called. "I will—"

A roar of falling waters filled the loudspeaker. For a second Refo's exalted face flickered on the screen. Came a click and the instrument went dead.

The ship's engines faltered and the nose started to come up. It steadied as Teraf adjusted the controls for a glide toward the Sais airport. Tenderly he slipped his arm around Pan's shaking shoulders and kissed her dark hair as the flier dropped swiftly.

L'Envoi

Chief: . . . You see the end of things.
The power of a thousand kings
Helped us to this, and now the power
Is so much hay that was a flower.
Lucius: We have been very great and strong.
Chief: *That's over now.*
Lucius: It will be long
Before the world will see our like.
Chief: We've kept the thieves beyond the dyke
A good long time, here on the wall . . .
Lucius: Colonel, we ought to sound a call
To make an end of this.
Chief: We ought.

Look—there's the hill-top where we fought
Old Foxfoot. Look—there in the whin.
Old ruffian knave! Come on. Fall in!

JOHN MASEFIELD'S *The Frontier.*

Athens.

Hermes to his friend Teraf—greetings and health.

Your messenger has just arrived, after more than a year of wandering over what is left of Arabia. The other messengers you speak of never got through.

Strange how distances stretch out now—into infinity. And time stretches too. Ten years since the flood! Great Land of Nod!

You ask me to visit you in Sais, but I fear that is impossible, though if things get worse here I may change my mind. They need me in Hellas, these queer people who have suddenly become very old and helpless; who dream of past greatness more and more as the years creep by.

We are established, as perhaps you have heard, on Mount Olympus, not far from Athens. We landed there safely just before the power failed. Your old capital was completely destroyed by the flood and the earthquakes and storms which followed. A new Athens has been built by refugees farther up in the mountains, but it is a sorry place made up mostly of stone huts and a few tottering temples. Perhaps in time . . .

Heracles has built a palace of sorts for the court on top of Olympus where it is easy to defend. Marble and all that, but no running water or electricity. Cockroaches in the kitchens! Bugs in the bedrooms! Terrible, in fact. I can't stand the place and am living in the proverbial vine-covered cottage half a league to the south. Have a wife now . . . a little girl from Attica. You'd like her.

I go up to the palace each week and publish my own version of *The Planet* . . . mostly a scandal sheet about court gossip. Put it out on a crazy flat-bed press I made myself. I preach the gospel of hope. . . . Tell them that communication soon will be restored and that the Anarchiate will send help—all that sort of rot. The fact is, of course, that the meteor belt shows no signs of clearing; not a ship can get through. And last week Mars stopped calling us. Our miserable radar station isn't strong enough to answer them, so the Anarchiate has sent through a message saying that, since no reply has been received from Earth since the flood, it is presumed that everyone in Atlan perished.

We're all finished, really, and I know it. But I feel so sorry for Zeus and the rest of them that I put on a brave face and scurry about acting as messenger and quartermaster for their eternal intrigues. The Hellenes tolerate me because they think I have a charmed life or something. But they call me a thief and block every effort I make to salvage machinery and other remnants of the old culture.

What few factories escaped the catastrophe are falling apart now. No power. The natives wear skins and eke out a miserable existence by farming the rocky valleys and raising sheep on the mountain slopes. What was the use of all that education they received under the empire? They make no use of it.

Athena, bless her soul, still has some influence over them. She tries to maintain a few schools. If you ask me, they are a waste of time, except that they keep her busy. She's really splendid, though. Perhaps I'm too pessimistic. Her simple teachings may make the Hellenes a great race in generations to come—if the barbarians don't finish them first.

I almost wish Heracles had let Zeus stay with Hephaestus. The Pitar isn't the man he used to be when you knew him. Grows a bit senile, poor chap. Has illusions that he is still ruler of Earth—when he is not planning how to restore the empire or winning new enemies among the populace by making love to the Hellenic girls.

Hera is fatter than ever, and just as jealous. Still has her receptions, although nobody but the Atlanteans go. But Zeus was right when he said he couldn't live without her. She waits on him hand and foot, now that attractive servants are hard to find.

Aphrodite has aged terribly, particularly since she has been replaced by Medea as official court vampire. Yes, the Argonauts escaped, even though their ship did crash on its way back to Atlan. All of them finally made their way here, where their good right arms have been much needed, I can tell you. Theseus is talking of having another Argo built so he can sail to Mexico after pitchblende with which to make orichalcum, but I doubt that anything will come of that. The last word we got from Chichen Itza was that the Aztecs were storming the city. Nothing since then. Of course, there are a few pitchblende deposits in the Caucasus. Maybe. . . .

Getting back to Medea, she leads Jason a sorry life due to the fact, I suppose, that she never became queen of Iberia after all. She also messes around with Egyptian spells, which don't work, and Egyptian poisons, which do. Lately she took a fancy to Heracles, but he couldn't be bothered, so I'm afraid he is in for trouble. Zeus has sent him to do some cleanup work around Hellas in order to get him out of harm's way for a while. I hear that he has greatly impressed the natives with his feats of strength.

Poor old Herc. He's a good civil engineer, of course, but what we need is a nuclear physicist—and electronics are just beyond him. Can't get the workings of an atomic pile through his big head. Sits and puzzles over plans, and talks about rebuilding Bab El, but it's all Hellenic to him. I try to help, but I'm a chronicler, not a chemist. The few real engineers who escaped from Bab El are not up to it either, without Hephaestus' help. How we miss the old man!

Thank Gaea and Chronus for Ares, though. He and most of his men managed to reach Crete on that last flight of warships. He's with us now, curt and authoritative as ever, but a real tower of strength when the natives threaten to get nasty.

Funny thing. The Hellenes have come to regard us as malignant supermen—almost as gods. So does the old order change. They hate us, though they respect us, thanks to Zeus' thunderbolts, as they call our guns. We brought enough orichalcum to charge those weapons for so long as we last, so I anticipate no real trouble.

The people have a sneaking admiration for Athena and Heracles but, strange to say, Refo has become their real idol. They've got the whole story twisted, somehow. He is no longer the misguided king who brought about the destruction of a world, but a demigod who strove with the high gods and failed. They've even given him a new name. Call him Prometheus, the forethinker.

They have carved a statue of him in chains on the mountain facing Olympus. Gruesome sight it is, with the vultures nesting around it. A constant reminder of our sorrows. The Hellenes say, of course, that the vultures are sent by Zeus to torture their hero.

All kinds of hocus pocus stories have been built around him. Refo is to return soon, they say, and lead his people back to the Golden Age. Solar myth stuff, you see, but I suppose it helps them forget their empty bellies.

Incidentally, I wouldn't advise you to visit Athens just now. You've become a solar myth too, my boy. The natives have you classified as the traitor who stole his brother's sweetheart and caused the latter's failure in his struggle to steal atomic fire from the gods. They think of you as being eternally bowed down by the weight of your misdeeds, so act accordingly if you should ever have to come here and wish to stay all in one piece. I might add that they've even changed your name to fit the story. You are now Epimetheus, the afterthinker. As for Pan Doh Ra . . . Well!

Glad to hear from your messenger that things are holding up so well in Egypt. You have a civilization there that you can sink your teeth into. It isn't much, compared to Atlantis, but it's better than this barbarian hole and may be able to carry the torch until civilization has a chance to recover from its shock, or until Mars gets through to us again. Just don't let the Arabs or the Ethiopians gobble you in the meantime.

Well, good luck. It's growing too dark to write and we have no electricity here. Give my love to Pan. I hope you won't be angry if I say that straight from the heart.

Farewell.

1—76